The Path to Truth...
or to Madness

VLAD SID

Copyright © [2024] Vlad Sid

Title: The Path to Truth... or to Madness

All rights reserved. No part of this publication may be reproduced, distributed, or transmitted in any form or by any means, including photocopying, recording, or other electronic or mechanical methods, without the prior written permission of the author, except in the case of brief quotations embodied in critical reviews and certain other noncommercial uses permitted by copyright law.

Disclaimer: The characters and events in this book are fictional. Any resemblance to actual persons, living or dead, or actual events is purely coincidental.

Chapter 1: The Discovery

The fog hung low over Briarwood as the first rays of dawn struggled to break through the dense, gray clouds. The old warehouse district was quiet, the kind of quiet that made the air feel heavy, as if it were holding its breath. Detective Evelyn Mercer stepped carefully over a broken chain-link fence, her boots crunching on shattered glass and crumbling brick. She moved with a practiced ease, scanning the scene with eyes that had grown accustomed to the darkness.

The call had come in an hour ago: a body found near an abandoned loading dock. The officer on duty had said there was something strange about the positioning, but nothing could have prepared Evelyn for what she saw.

The body sat slumped in a rusted metal chair, arms draped over the sides like a broken marionette. The victim's eyes were half-open, gazing into the empty space ahead, as if they had been caught mid-thought in the last moments of life. There were no immediate signs of violence—no blood, no obvious injuries. And yet, something about the scene felt…off.

Evelyn crouched down beside the body, her breath misting in the cool air. She noticed a faint bruise on the left side of the neck and the peculiar way the victim's fingers curled inward. A broken watch adorned the wrist, its glass cracked, and the hands were frozen at 4:17.

"Detective Mercer?" A young officer's voice broke the silence.

She glanced up. "What have we got?"

The officer hesitated, glancing at the victim. "The initial report suggested a heart attack, but there's this…" He pointed to the left hand, where an intricate pattern had been carved into the palm. The lines formed a symbol that Evelyn didn't recognize—something almost geometric, yet disturbingly organic in its shape.

As she leaned in closer, she caught a faint sound behind her. A shuffle, like a foot scraping against gravel. Her eyes darted to the edge of the alleyway, where a small figure stood, half-hidden in the fog.

A child. A boy, no older than nine, with wide eyes and a pale face.

Evelyn stood slowly, not wanting to scare him. "Hey there," she called softly. "It's okay. I'm not going to hurt you."

The boy took a step back, clutching something tightly to his chest. "He said it was for the angels," he whispered, his voice trembling. "He told me not to look."

Before she could ask anything else, the boy turned and vanished into the mist.

Evelyn stared after him, a chill creeping up her spine. She returned her attention to the victim, her gaze settling on the torn note sticking out of the pocket. She unfolded it carefully, her eyes narrowing at the words written in neat, slanted handwriting: *"In the quiet places, we find our truth."*

As she stood there, the sound of her phone ringing shattered the stillness. She answered, only to be met with silence, then a voice—distorted and low: "You're looking in the wrong place."

The line went dead.

Evelyn pocketed her phone, her jaw tightening. This was no accident, no chance encounter. She could feel it, deep in her bones.

Something far darker was at play in Briarwood.

Chapter 2: Threads of Mystery

The steady hum of the precinct buzzed around Evelyn as she sat at her desk, sifting through the initial report. It was nearly noon, but the fog outside still lingered, casting a dull gray light through the narrow windows. The note recovered from the victim's pocket lay in front of her, the phrase "In the quiet places, we find our truth" seeming to taunt her from the paper.

She'd run the victim's prints and ID through the system, and his name came back: Harold Falkner, a local artist known for his abstract sculptures, many of which dotted Briarwood's parks and galleries. Falkner had no known enemies and no history of trouble with the law. He was an odd choice for a target, which made his death all the more perplexing.

Evelyn tapped a pen against her notepad. The symbol carved into his palm kept coming back to her—a detail so precise that it couldn't have been done without a steady hand. It looked almost ritualistic, yet didn't match any symbols she was familiar with. And then there was the child, as the police later found out, his name was Tommy.. His words, "He said it was for the angels," played in her mind on a loop. What had he seen? Who was "he"?

Evelyn's thoughts were interrupted by a familiar voice.

"Morning, Mercer." Adam Whitfield's tone was casual, but his eyes were sharp as he leaned against her desk. "Heard you found something interesting in the old district. A little different from your usual cases, isn't it?"

Evelyn raised an eyebrow. "What brings you here, Whitfield? Fishing for a story?"

"Maybe," he admitted with a half-smirk. "Or maybe I'm just curious. Harold Falkner wasn't exactly a big name, but his art had its admirers. Strange way for an artist to go, don't you think?"

She eyed him, assessing whether he knew more than he was letting on. "What do you know about Falkner?"

"Not much," Adam replied, crossing his arms. "Except that his latest exhibit was called *Quiet Places*. It opened last month, featuring a series of sculptures inspired by…something he said he dreamed about." He tilted his head slightly. "Sound familiar?"

Evelyn felt a prickle of interest. *Quiet Places*. The phrase connected too well to the note in Falkner's pocket. "I wasn't aware of the exhibit," she said, keeping her tone measured. "Any idea where I can find more about it?"

"There's a small gallery downtown," Adam said. "The owner's a friend of mine. I could introduce you."

She hesitated for a moment. Letting Adam get involved in her investigation was risky, especially with their history. But then again, any lead was better than none, and Adam had a knack for uncovering things others missed.

"Alright," she agreed. "Let's go."

The Gallery

The downtown gallery was nestled in an older part of the city, surrounded by brick facades and faded murals. Inside, the walls were lined with Falkner's sculptures, each piece jagged and abstract, their dark metal surfaces gleaming under the dim lighting.

The gallery owner, Lydia Burns, greeted them. She was a petite woman with silver-streaked hair and an air of quiet authority. "Adam, always a pleasure," she said, then turned to Evelyn with a polite smile. "Detective Mercer, I presume? Adam mentioned you were looking into Harold's work."

Evelyn nodded. "Yes. I'm trying to understand if there's any connection between his art and his death. Can you tell me more about this exhibit?"

Lydia led them to a central piece in the room, a large sculpture composed of twisted metal, its shape suggestive of wings folded around an invisible figure. "This is the centerpiece of *Quiet Places,*" she explained. "Harold said it represented the spaces we retreat to when we need solace. He believed there was something sacred about silence, almost…spiritual."

Evelyn studied the sculpture, noticing a familiar pattern etched along its base—the same geometric lines she'd seen carved into Falkner's palm. Her pulse quickened. "Did Harold ever mention being threatened or having unusual visitors?" she asked.

Lydia's expression grew serious. "A few weeks ago, a man came to the gallery. He was…odd. He asked a lot of questions about Harold's work, especially this exhibit. I remember Harold seemed uneasy afterward."

"Do you know the man's name?" Adam interjected.

"I'm afraid not," Lydia replied, shaking her head. "But he wore a distinctive silver ring, with some sort of insignia. It looked like a pair of crossed feathers."

Evelyn exchanged a glance with Adam. The crossed feathers felt like a lead worth pursuing. But as they turned to leave the gallery, her phone buzzed with a new message.

It was an untraceable number again, and the message read: *He's closer than you think.*

Chapter 3: Whispers in the Dark

The late afternoon light filtered through the tall windows of Briarwood's police headquarters, casting long shadows across Evelyn's desk. The message from the untraceable number gnawed at her thoughts: *He's closer than you think.* Whoever was sending these, they were clearly tracking her progress. It wasn't just taunting; it was a warning. But from whom?

Evelyn had spent the last hour combing through Falkner's background for any anomalies—arrests, lawsuits, enemies. But his record was spotless. It was as though the artist had lived an unremarkably quiet life, making his death seem even more out of place.

Her thoughts were interrupted by the sound of footsteps approaching. Evelyn glanced up to see her colleague, Detective Marcus Hale, a tall, broad-shouldered man with a gruff demeanor, leaning against the doorway.

"Heard you've got a strange one on your hands," Hale said, his tone a mix of curiosity and skepticism.

"You could say that." Evelyn's voice was guarded. She trusted Hale, but she preferred to keep her cards close. "Anything I should know?"

"Actually, yes," he replied, crossing his arms. "You asked me to look into Harold Falkner's contacts. Turns out, he made a couple of large, unexplained cash withdrawals over the last three months—each about two weeks apart. No records showing where the money went."

Evelyn's brow furrowed. Falkner wasn't known to be in debt, nor was he a gambler. "How much money are we talking?"

"Close to fifty thousand," Hale answered. "Doesn't exactly scream starving artist, does it?"

She shook her head. "Any chance this has to do with the man who visited him at the gallery?"

"That's what I'm thinking," Hale said. "I'm running down the CCTV footage from the area, but no luck so far. The cameras there are old, barely functioning."

"Keep on it," she replied. "I've got a feeling there's more to this."

The Streets of Briarwood

Evelyn decided to pay a visit to the rougher side of town, where Tommy Lancaster lived. The neighborhood was run-down, with peeling paint and boarded-up windows. She found his apartment easily enough—a small, dingy building at the end of a narrow street. She knocked on the door, and after a few moments, a weary-looking woman in her thirties opened it.

"Detective Mercer," Evelyn introduced herself. "I'm here to talk to Tommy."

The woman's face tightened. "He's not home," she said defensively. "He's at school."

Evelyn could sense the tension in her voice. "I understand. I just wanted to follow up about the other morning. Tommy was near a crime scene, and I need to make sure he's okay."

The woman hesitated, then reluctantly opened the door wider. "Come in," she said. "We can talk inside."

The apartment was cluttered but clean. Tommy's mother, Rachel Lancaster, gestured to the worn-out couch. "Tommy hasn't been the same since that day," she confessed, sitting across from Evelyn. "He keeps talking about 'the man with the silver ring.'"

Evelyn's pulse quickened. "What did he say about the man?"

Rachel's eyes darted toward the closed bedroom door. "Tommy said the man was following Harold before he died. He saw him a few times near the gallery and outside our building. He said…he saw him talking to Harold the night before it happened."

Evelyn felt a chill run through her. "Did Tommy mention anything else?"

Rachel shook her head. "Just that the man told him not to look. I don't know what my son saw, but he's been having nightmares. He says…he hears whispering in his room at night."

Researching the Silver Ring

Back at the precinct, Evelyn searched databases and records for any connection to a silver ring with crossed feathers. After hours of dead ends, she found a name: The Brotherhood of the Feather, an old, secretive group once known for their involvement in questionable rituals and underground activities.

There was no recent activity associated with the group; most references dated back over a decade. But they were believed to have operated in Briarwood at one time, meeting in obscure places like abandoned churches and old mansions. It was unclear if they were still active or had simply faded into the city's shadows.

Evelyn leaned back in her chair, her mind racing. Could the Brotherhood be connected to Falkner's death? And if so, what was the motive? She wasn't even sure if the group still existed, but the symbol on the ring was too similar to ignore.

As she pondered her next move, her phone buzzed again. Another message from the untraceable number: *He isn't the first. He won't be the last.*

Chapter 4: Hidden Faces

The crisp night air was laced with a biting chill as Evelyn stood outside the dimly lit church on the outskirts of Briarwood. The building, a relic from the 19th century, had long been abandoned. Its stone walls were covered in creeping ivy, and the stained glass windows were cracked, their colors faded by time. She had tracked down one of the rumored meeting places of the Brotherhood of the Feather, following a lead about an old caretaker who might know something about the group's activities.

She entered cautiously, her flashlight cutting a path through the darkness. The interior was eerily quiet, with dust motes floating in the air. She spotted movement at the back of the sanctuary—a hunched figure sweeping the floor.

"Excuse me," she called out, her voice echoing off the stone walls. "I'm Detective Mercer. I'm looking for information about a group called the Brotherhood of the Feather."

The old man, Father Jonathan, stopped sweeping and turned toward her. His face was lined with deep wrinkles, and his eyes held a look of weariness that came from too many years spent in the company of secrets. "The Brotherhood?"

he murmured, his voice gravelly. "They're nothing but whispers now. Shadows of the past."

"But they were real," Evelyn pressed. "I found a symbol—crossed feathers—linked to their name. I need to know if they're still active."

Father Jonathan hesitated, his gaze drifting to a series of carvings on the wall. They were faint, nearly obscured by age, but Evelyn could make out the shapes: two feathers crossing over a circle. "They disbanded years ago," he said slowly. "But some remnants remain. They were…obsessed with transformation. With finding enlightenment through darkness."

Evelyn's grip tightened on the flashlight. "What kind of darkness?"

The old priest's voice grew quiet, almost reverent. "Rituals. Sacrifices, of a sort. Not in the physical sense, but in the mind. They believed in crossing boundaries that shouldn't be crossed, using art and symbols as gateways."

"Did Harold Falkner have any ties to them?" Evelyn asked.

"Falkner?" Father Jonathan's brow furrowed. "Yes, I knew him. He was fascinated by the old stories, by the idea of hidden truths. He came here a few months ago, asking about the Brotherhood. Said he had been seeing things in his dreams…visions he couldn't explain."

Evelyn felt the pieces starting to fall into place. "And this man with the silver ring? Do you know who he is?"

Father Jonathan's expression darkened. "A name long forgotten. But if the ring is still being worn, then the Brotherhood's shadows haven't entirely vanished."

An Unexpected Visit

Later that night, Evelyn returned to her apartment, her mind racing with the implications of what Father Jonathan had revealed. As she walked through the door, a sense of unease settled over her. The lights were off, but there was something different—an odd silence, a feeling that she wasn't alone.

She reached for her gun, but before she could draw it, a figure emerged from the darkness—a man in a long coat, wearing a silver ring with crossed feathers. His face was partially obscured by the shadows.

"Detective Mercer," he said in a calm, almost friendly voice. "You've been asking the wrong questions."

Evelyn's pulse raced, but she kept her composure. "Who are you?" she demanded. "What do you want?"

"That's not the question you should be asking," he replied, stepping closer. "The real question is: What did Harold Falkner discover that got him killed?"

Evelyn kept her gun trained on him. "Why don't you tell me?"

He smiled faintly. "It's not something I can explain. It's something you have to see for yourself." With that, he turned and walked toward the open window. "You're not far off, Detective. But if you keep digging, you might not like what you find."

Before Evelyn could react, he climbed out and disappeared into the night, leaving her with more questions than answers.

Revisiting the Gallery

The next day, Evelyn returned to the gallery, her thoughts on the mysterious man's cryptic words. As she walked through the doors, Lydia Burns greeted her, but there was a tension in the air.

"Detective, you should see this," Lydia said, leading Evelyn to a back room where some of Harold Falkner's private sketches were kept. She pulled out a large notebook, its pages filled with drawings of shapes, patterns, and symbols. Among them was the same geometric design that had been carved into Falkner's palm.

But one sketch stood out: it was a rough depiction of a place—a narrow alleyway lined with old brick walls, a hidden door at the far end. Scrawled beneath the drawing were the words: *Enter through darkness, find the quiet place.*

Evelyn felt a shiver run down her spine. The sketch looked familiar. It was an alley not far from where Falkner's body had been found.

The Hidden Door

As evening fell, Evelyn found herself standing at the entrance of the alleyway depicted in Falkner's sketch. She walked cautiously toward the door at the far end, a sense of dread building with each step. The door was old, its wood cracked and weathered, but it wasn't locked.

She pushed it open and stepped inside.

The room beyond was small and dimly lit, filled with old furniture and canvases covered in draped cloths. In the center of the room sat an easel, holding a half-finished painting. Evelyn pulled back the cloth to reveal a chilling sight: the painting depicted a figure slumped in a chair—Falkner himself. The details were eerily precise, down to the broken watch and the carved symbol on his palm.

There was only one difference: in the background, barely visible, stood a shadowy figure wearing a silver ring.

As she examined the painting more closely, a soft sound echoed from the corner—a faint whisper, just like Tommy had described.

Evelyn turned, her flashlight cutting through the darkness. But the room was empty.

Chapter 5: Tangled Paths

Evelyn's investigation seemed to be unraveling as much as it was progressing. Every clue she found only seemed to lead to more questions. The gallery, the old church, the Brotherhood of the Feather—it all felt connected, yet none of it fit together neatly. The sketch of the alleyway and the painting depicting Falkner's death had rattled her, but they also felt staged, as if she were being led to find them.

She couldn't ignore the feeling that she was being manipulated. But by whom?

A Conflicting Clue

Back at the precinct, Hale had managed to track down some CCTV footage from near Falkner's gallery on the night of his death. The footage was grainy, but it showed a figure in a dark coat, roughly matching the description of the man with the silver ring. However, a second figure appeared later—a woman in a red scarf, lingering near the gallery after Falkner was last seen alive.

Evelyn paused the footage and zoomed in on the woman's face, but the quality made it hard to identify her. "Who is she?" she murmured, mostly to herself.

"Maybe an accomplice?" Hale suggested, peering over her shoulder.

"Or maybe just a red herring," Evelyn replied. "But we need to find her, just in case."

The search for the woman with the red scarf took a frustrating turn when a witness report came in, claiming that a different person—an older man with a limp—had been seen near Falkner's apartment the night before his death. The more they dug, the more possibilities emerged, none of them conclusive.

An Unplanned Encounter with Adam

Feeling overwhelmed by the lack of clear answers, Evelyn decided to take a break at the local café, a place she often visited when she needed to think. As she sipped her coffee, Adam Whitfield slid into the seat across from her, his expression a mix of concern and curiosity.

"You look like you could use a distraction," he said.

"Or a lead that isn't going in circles," she muttered.

Adam leaned back, his eyes studying her. "You know, I've been following up on some things myself," he said, casually. "I found out that Falkner wasn't just an artist—he was also collecting stories. He interviewed people who claimed to have had strange experiences in Briarwood—people who saw things they couldn't explain."

"Like the man in Tommy's story?" Evelyn asked, her interest piqued.

Adam nodded. "Or the whispers he heard at night. Falkner was interested in these so-called 'thin places,' where the line between reality and…something else is blurred."

Evelyn couldn't help but notice the way Adam's gaze lingered on her, as if reading her reaction. It wasn't the first time he'd looked at her that way, and she wasn't entirely sure how she felt about it. There was a history between them—a time when things had nearly become more than professional—but she had pulled back, fearing complications.

"You think Falkner was killed because of what he was investigating?" she asked, keeping her tone neutral.

"Maybe," Adam replied, his voice lowering. "Or maybe it's more personal than that. I think you're closer to this than you realize, Evelyn."

Their eyes met, and she felt a subtle pull toward him, the kind that came from shared secrets and unresolved tension. But she quickly broke eye contact, shifting the conversation back to the case.

A New Victim

The next morning, another body was found. The victim, Eleanor Cross, was a local historian who specialized in Briarwood's more obscure folklore. Her death bore no immediate resemblance to Falkner's—the cause was blunt force trauma, and there were no strange symbols or notes—but something about the timing felt deliberate.

Evelyn and Hale arrived at the scene, where they were briefed by the responding officers. Hale was the first to voice the obvious. "It doesn't fit the pattern," he said. "But it's too close to the first case to be ignored."

Evelyn knelt beside the body, examining the surroundings. There were papers scattered around—a research project on Briarwood's old legends. One of the documents was a printout of an interview…with Harold Falkner.

As she sifted through the documents, a familiar phrase caught her eye: *In the quiet places, we find our truth.*

A False Trail

With the second murder, the pressure was mounting to find a connection. Evelyn began tracing Eleanor's contacts, uncovering that she had recently corresponded with several people linked to Falkner's artistic circles. One name stood out—Martin Wilkes, a writer who had collaborated with Falkner on a few projects. Rumors suggested he had a history of mental instability and was obsessed with occult themes.

Evelyn and Hale paid Wilkes a visit, finding him in a cluttered apartment filled with books and strange artifacts. Wilkes was eccentric, rambling about "places that bleed" and "visions that consume." He claimed to know about the Brotherhood of the Feather, but when pressed, his answers were incoherent, blending fact and fiction in a way that made it impossible to determine if he was a genuine suspect or just a delusional man with a fascination for dark tales.

The deeper they dug, the more Evelyn began to suspect that Wilkes was another dead end. But just as she was about to dismiss him entirely, he muttered something that caught her off guard: "Harold and Eleanor…they weren't the first. And they won't be the last."

Chapter 6: Echoes of the Past

The feeling of chaos only seemed to deepen as Evelyn sat at her desk, poring over the documents from Eleanor Cross's apartment. The connections between the victims weren't clear, but a deeper look at Eleanor's research showed she had been studying not just folklore but actual cold cases—unsolved murders dating back decades. Some of the cases involved mysterious symbols and unexplained circumstances, echoing details from Falkner's death.

But why would a historian have been researching these cases now? Evelyn wondered if someone had wanted to keep those stories buried.

A Breakthrough with Adam

Later that evening, Evelyn met Adam for a drink at their usual spot, a quiet bar on the edge of town. She needed to unwind but also wanted to see if Adam could help her make sense of the new information. There was an unspoken understanding between them; their conversations always straddled the line between personal and professional.

"I've been looking into those old cases," Adam said as he took a seat across from her. "It's strange. Some of them involve people who vanished without a trace. And there's something else…they were all artists, writers, or scholars. People who delved into the unknown."

"Like Falkner and Eleanor," Evelyn said, the pieces starting to fall into place. "You think someone's targeting people who look too closely?"

"Or maybe it's the places themselves," Adam replied, his tone almost conspiratorial. "Briarwood has always had an undercurrent of strange events. What if these murders are just echoes of something that's been here all along?"

The intensity in his gaze made her heart skip a beat. She wanted to ask more about his interest in the case, but she was also hesitant to blur the lines further. Instead, she leaned back, trying to appear unfazed. "And what about you, Adam? You seem pretty invested in this."

He smiled faintly. "Let's just say I have a personal fascination with things that don't have simple explanations."

There it was—another hint at something he wasn't telling her. Evelyn decided to change the subject, unwilling to push him just yet. "There's something else," she said, sliding a folder across the table. "I found a connection between Falkner and Eleanor. A name—Samuel Graves. He was a patron at the gallery and funded some of Falkner's projects."

Adam's expression shifted subtly, almost as if he recognized the name. "I've heard of him," he said slowly. "Wealthy, old family, likes to keep a low profile. But if Graves is involved, that could be a whole new direction. He's connected to a lot of influential people."

Samuel Graves' Estate

The next day, Evelyn and Hale paid a visit to Samuel Graves, whose estate sat on the outskirts of Briarwood, nestled behind wrought iron gates and surrounded by dense woods. The mansion was imposing, a relic from the early 1900s, with ivy climbing the stone walls and a sense of history that bordered on the unsettling.

Graves himself was in his late seventies, but his sharp eyes belied his age. He greeted the detectives with an air of politeness, though his voice carried a hint of skepticism. "What is this about, Detective?" he asked, ushering them into a grand study filled with old books and art.

"We're looking into the deaths of Harold Falkner and Eleanor Cross," Evelyn began, watching for his reaction. "Both of them had some kind of connection to you, directly or indirectly."

Graves raised an eyebrow. "Harold was an interesting artist. I supported some of his work, yes. And as for Eleanor, I believe she consulted with me on a few historical matters years ago. But I hardly knew either of them well."

"Did they ever mention anything unusual?" Hale pressed. "Any concerns or strange occurrences?"

Graves chuckled dryly. "This is Briarwood, Detective. There's always something strange happening. But I assure you, I had no involvement with whatever happened to them."

As they left the estate, Evelyn felt a lingering sense of unease. Graves had been charming, but there was a distance in his demeanor—a practiced detachment that made her suspect he was hiding more than he let on.

A Third Victim

Just as Evelyn began digging deeper into Graves' past, a third victim emerged: Lucas Hale, Marcus Hale's younger brother, was found dead under bizarre circumstances. Lucas had been known around town as a musician who played in local bars, but his death didn't appear related to the previous victims. There were no symbols, no cryptic messages—just a simple, tragic accident. Or at least that's how it seemed.

The connection felt tenuous at first, but Lucas had recently been seen at an art exhibition featuring Falkner's work. Evelyn started to wonder if there was an invisible thread linking these deaths—a kind of ripple effect, where seemingly unrelated events triggered a chain reaction of violence.

Marcus Hale's grief added a new layer of tension. He became more aggressive in pursuing leads, often clashing with Evelyn over the direction of the investigation. The case was no longer just a professional obligation; it had become personal, clouding his judgment and adding pressure to solve it quickly.

Uncovering More False Trails

As the investigation continued, Evelyn and Adam discovered more inconsistencies and confusing details. Witnesses who claimed to have seen important events contradicted each other. The woman in the red scarf was tracked down, only to turn out to be an out-of-town tourist who had nothing to do with the murders. Clues seemed to lead in circles—each time they thought they were close to an answer, the solution slipped through their fingers.

One evening, as Evelyn was going over case files in her apartment, she found an old letter tucked into one of Falkner's notebooks. It was addressed to an unknown recipient and spoke of "finding the key to unlock the truth in the quiet places." The letter was unsigned, but it was dated two years ago.

As she studied the letter, her phone buzzed with a message from an untraceable number: *You're looking in the wrong places. The truth isn't where you think it is.*

Chapter 7: Shadows from the Past

The case had begun to feel like a labyrinth, but Evelyn was determined to keep pressing forward. The discovery of the old letter and the mysterious text message left her with an uneasy feeling, as if someone was playing a game and she was just a pawn. But who? And why?

A Glimpse into Evelyn's Past

As Evelyn sat in her dimly lit apartment, combing through files, a faded photograph slipped from the stack of papers. It was an old photo of her with her father, taken when she was about eight years old, both of them smiling outside a small cottage by a lake. The sight of it triggered a memory she hadn't thought of in years.

Flashback: Evelyn, Age 8

The smell of pine and lake water filled the air as young Evelyn wandered outside the family cottage. Her father was fixing the old rowboat, as he always did on weekends. But something else had caught her eye—a strange figure, standing in the distance near the tree line, just far enough away that she couldn't make out the details. When she blinked, the figure was gone.

"Evelyn!" her father's voice broke the silence. "Come help me with this."

She ran toward him, forgetting about the figure. But years later, after he died in an unsolved accident, she remembered that moment.

Adam's Secrets Begin to Surface

The next day, Evelyn met with Adam to go over the latest leads. As they talked, she noticed something in his voice, a subtle hesitation when he mentioned Samuel Graves. She had never asked much about Adam's past, but now she felt the need to know more.

"You seem to know a lot about Graves," Evelyn said, watching him closely.

Adam's gaze dropped to the table. "My father…he used to work for the Graves family. He handled some of their legal affairs. I wasn't exactly close to my dad, but I heard things." He paused, as if debating whether to say more. "There were rumors about the family being involved in strange business deals and…other things. It's probably nothing."

But Evelyn sensed there was more to the story than he was letting on.

Flashback: Adam, Age 17

Adam stood outside his father's study, listening to the muffled conversation inside. He was never allowed in when "business" was being discussed. Through the crack in the door, he caught sight of Samuel Graves—an intimidating figure even then—gesturing toward a folder on the desk.

"Keep this quiet," Graves said. "We don't need anyone digging into the past."

Adam had never forgotten the tone in Graves' voice—cold and final. It was the first time he realized his father's work wasn't just about legal documents and contracts.

Hale's Struggle with Loss

Marcus Hale had thrown himself into his work with a renewed intensity, but the grief over his brother's death gnawed at him. Evelyn could see it in his eyes—a haunted look that hadn't been there before. She knew he was on edge, and it was affecting his judgment.

"Hale," she said softly, catching him before he stormed out of the precinct one night. "You can talk to me, you know."

Hale's jaw tightened. "It's nothing. Just…Lucas didn't deserve to go out like that."

"None of them did," she replied, her voice low. "But we'll get to the bottom of this."

Flashback: Hale, Age 15

Lucas, two years younger than Marcus, was always the troublemaker. But Marcus had been the one to protect him, to cover for him whenever he got into a scrape. He remembered a night when Lucas had disappeared for hours, only to be found at a local park, half-conscious and scared out of his mind. Lucas had mumbled about seeing "shadows that moved" and hearing voices that seemed to come from the trees.

It was just a childish imagination, or so Marcus had thought. But now, as he faced his brother's mysterious death, he couldn't shake the feeling that there had been a pattern all along—a history of events connected to Briarwood's darker side.

Another False Trail

As Evelyn followed up on more leads about Samuel Graves, she discovered an unexpected detail. Graves had recently made a large donation to a psychiatric facility in a nearby town. Curious, she reached out to the facility and found that he had been funding the treatment of a specific patient—Anna Hargrove, a former artist who had exhibited work at Falkner's gallery years ago.

Anna had suffered a mental breakdown and had been institutionalized ever since, but there were records suggesting she had been working on a project involving the same crossed feathers symbol that Evelyn had found connected to the Brotherhood of the Feather.

When Evelyn visited Anna, she found a woman who spoke in riddles, her mind fragmented by years of trauma. "The Feather doesn't fly," Anna murmured as she stared at the wall. "It falls. And when it touches the ground, it opens the door."

Evelyn left the facility more confused than ever, but also with a sense of dread. What if the connection wasn't the killers themselves, but the places they left behind—places where reality felt thin, where people like Falkner, Eleanor, and Anna had been drawn for reasons even they couldn't fully understand?

Chapter 8: The Unseen Threads

Evelyn's mind buzzed with possibilities, each clue only serving to tangle the web further. The cryptic words of Anna Hargrove, Samuel Graves' elusive answers, and Adam's fragmented past all pointed toward something much bigger than she'd initially suspected. Yet the real connection remained just out of reach, like a shadow that moved at the edge of her vision.

A New Discovery About Evelyn

The more Evelyn dug into the case, the more she found herself remembering things she had long pushed aside—things about her own family. Her father's unsolved hit-and-run had never quite made sense to her, especially given his profession as a historian who specialized in folklore. She wondered now if he had stumbled onto something in Briarwood's dark past, something that had cost him his life.

As Evelyn researched her father's old notes, she came across references to a series of obscure writings on "thin places"—geographical spots where the barrier between the natural and supernatural was supposedly weaker. One of those places was near Briarwood's old forest, not far from the lake where she had seen the mysterious figure as a child. Her father's notes hinted at strange occurrences there, things he had planned to investigate further before his death.

Flashback: Evelyn, Age 14

Evelyn remembered sitting by the lake, clutching her father's journal after the funeral. She had opened it to a page marked with a single word: *Veil*. Below it, her father had written, *In Briarwood, the veil is thin, but beware the places that seem to call for you.* She had never understood what it meant, but now, in the midst of the murders and cryptic symbols, the words took on a chilling significance.

Adam's Search for Answers

Adam, driven by the need to understand the truth, began looking into his father's old dealings with the Graves family. He knew his father had left behind boxes of documents in the attic of the house where Adam had grown up, and he decided to take a trip back there to search for answers.

As he sifted through the dusty papers, Adam found a series of letters written by Samuel Graves to his father. They referenced a "failed experiment" and a "lost key," along with payments for keeping certain records sealed. One of the letters, however, contained a detail that made his blood run cold: *If Evelyn had known about this, she would have never let you walk away, Richard. Some doors are meant to stay closed.*

The implication was clear: Evelyn's family and the Graves had a shared history, one that had been deliberately hidden.

Flashback: Adam, Age 10

Adam remembered being taken to the Graves mansion by his father one winter afternoon. He had been left in the study, where an old, leather-bound book lay open on the desk. The pages were filled with diagrams and strange symbols that made no sense to him at the time. Samuel Graves had appeared moments later, quietly closing the book and asking Adam if he knew how to keep secrets. The memory had seemed unimportant for years, but now he wondered if it was the beginning of his connection to the darkness unfolding around him.

Hale's Pursuit of the Truth

Marcus Hale was unraveling, his brother's death eating away at him. He threw himself into investigating the background of the victims, convinced there had to be a pattern they were missing. He found that Lucas had been involved in more than just music; he had been working on a documentary about the myths surrounding Briarwood, including some disturbing tales of people vanishing in the woods.

As Hale pieced together Lucas's research, he found a series of photographs taken near an old stone circle in the forest.

One image showed a faint figure in the background, barely visible but definitely there—a man with a silver ring, the same detail described by witnesses near Falkner's gallery.

Flashback: Hale, Age 22

Marcus had once gone hiking in those very woods with Lucas, who had joked about "ghosts" living there. Lucas had found a peculiar stone that he claimed was a marker for some old ritual, laughing off Marcus's suggestion to leave it alone. Hale had forgotten about it until now, but the picture brought the memory flooding back. Was his brother's interest in the forest more than just curiosity?

The Appearance of a Mysterious Witness

Evelyn's investigation took a surprising turn when a man named Daniel Croft came forward, claiming to have information about the murders. He had been living off the grid for years, keeping to himself in a cabin deep in the woods. Croft spoke of seeing strange lights at night and hearing voices that weren't there. He had seen Falkner once, wandering near his cabin before his death, muttering about needing to "cross the threshold."

Evelyn was intrigued but skeptical. "And you didn't think to report this sooner?" she asked, her voice edged with disbelief.

"I didn't think anyone would believe me," Croft replied. "But I've seen things around Briarwood—things that don't add up. I think the deaths are connected to that old place in the woods. There's something buried there, something that's waking up."

Evelyn felt a chill as Croft described an old ruin near the stone circle that Hale had mentioned. It matched the places her father had been researching before his death. Could all of this be pointing toward something ancient and malignant, hidden beneath the surface of Briarwood?

Chapter 9: Beneath the Surface

The weight of the case pressed heavily on Evelyn, Adam, and Hale, as if the mystery itself was tightening its grip on them. Each day brought more questions, and with every step forward, there seemed to be a step back. The investigation was starting to feel less like solving a puzzle and more like unraveling a story that had begun long before they arrived.

Evelyn's Growing Doubts

Evelyn sat in her office, staring at the scattered files across her desk. She was beginning to notice a strange pattern in the statements from witnesses—minor contradictions and gaps in memory. It was almost as if people were intentionally misremembering details. There was a frustrating vagueness to the accounts, which only deepened her suspicion that someone was influencing the narrative.

Her thoughts drifted to Adam. There was something about him—an intensity that drew her in but also unsettled her. She wondered if his interest in the case was purely professional or if it was driven by something deeper, perhaps a need to confront his own past.

Evelyn's Inner Conflict

Evelyn had always prided herself on staying objective, but this case was different. She found herself drawn to the history of Briarwood, to the whispers of strange happenings. It was personal in a way she couldn't entirely understand, as if the town's secrets resonated with something in her own past. The more she learned, the more she felt like she was trying to solve a riddle left behind by her father.

Adam's Increasing Involvement

Adam found himself spending more time at the precinct, offering insights and poring over files alongside Evelyn. As he helped her track down leads, their conversations began to stray beyond the case, revealing pieces of Adam's life he rarely spoke about.

"I wasn't always in Briarwood," he admitted one evening as they went through files. "I traveled a lot when I was younger. After my father died, I just…needed to get away."

"Why did you come back?" Evelyn asked, sensing there was more to the story.

Adam hesitated, his eyes focused on a photograph of the stone circle in the woods. "Sometimes you can't escape where you come from. Briarwood has a way of pulling people back. There are things I still don't understand—things that happened here when I was a kid. I guess I needed answers, too."

Adam's Dual Nature

Adam's voice held a quiet intensity, a mixture of curiosity and restraint. Evelyn could see that he was more than just a consultant helping with the case; he was invested in a way that hinted at a personal quest. It wasn't just about finding the killer—it was about confronting the past, even if it meant facing the shadows lurking in his own life.

Hale's Fraying Nerves

Marcus Hale had grown more withdrawn since his brother's death, but it didn't escape Evelyn's notice that he was also more driven, almost obsessively so. He had taken to spending long hours in the precinct's basement archive, digging through old case files in search of any clue that could tie the current murders to something from the past.

One evening, Evelyn found him there, surrounded by stacks of yellowed reports. "Hale, you're going to drive yourself crazy if you keep this up," she said gently. "We can't solve it all at once."

Hale looked up, exhaustion evident in his eyes. "It's not just about solving the case," he replied, his voice hoarse. "I need to understand why Lucas died. Why all of this is happening. It feels like there's a pattern, but I can't see it clearly."

Hale's Desperation

Hale's determination to find answers was fueled by more than professional duty; it was deeply personal. His brother's death had reopened old wounds, forcing him to confront feelings of helplessness that he had buried for years. Now, as the investigation progressed, it wasn't just about catching a killer—it was about proving to himself that he could protect the people he cared about.

Revisiting Anna Hargrove

Evelyn decided to revisit Anna Hargrove at the psychiatric facility, hoping to glean more information. This time, she brought Adam along, thinking his presence might help draw out some new detail. As they entered Anna's room, they found her sketching on a scrap of paper—crude drawings of birds with broken wings and feathers falling like rain.

Evelyn approached slowly, her voice soft. "Anna, do you remember talking to me about the Feather? You mentioned a door."

Anna glanced up, her eyes unfocused. "The Feather…falls and rises," she whispered, her voice thin. "It doesn't come alone. It brings the others with it."

Adam leaned closer. "Who are the others, Anna? What do they want?"

Anna's gaze sharpened suddenly, and she clutched the sketch to her chest. "They watch. They wait for the right time," she murmured, her voice dropping to a conspiratorial tone. "The veil thins when the moon is dark."

The words lingered in the air, casting a sense of unease. As they left the facility, Evelyn couldn't shake the feeling that Anna was more than just a victim of circumstance. There was a strange clarity to her madness, as if she was a witness to a truth that lay just out of reach.

Chapter 10: The Weight of Secrets

The investigation had become a test of patience and perseverance, with Evelyn, Adam, and Hale each navigating their own paths through the darkness. As new clues emerged, they found themselves entangled not only in the case but in their own unresolved pasts. The secrets they kept from each other and from themselves were beginning to surface, and Briarwood seemed to whisper with every step they took.

Evelyn and the Veil

Evelyn couldn't shake Anna's cryptic words about the veil thinning. As she combed through her father's notes on "thin places," she began to notice other details that struck her as oddly familiar—locations in Briarwood that she had visited as a child, places her father had taken her on weekend trips under the guise of "adventure." She remembered a particular clearing in the woods, near the old stone circle, where she had found a peculiar symbol carved into a tree. It was the same crossed-feathers pattern she had seen connected to the Brotherhood.

Determined to follow this thread, Evelyn ventured out to the clearing. The air was heavy with the scent of damp earth, and the silence was almost oppressive. As she examined the tree, she noticed fresh scratches near the carved symbol, as if someone had recently disturbed the area. Nearby, she found an old charm bracelet lying half-buried in the dirt, its tiny metal charms shaped like feathers.

Evelyn's Growing Fear

For the first time in years, Evelyn felt a shiver of fear. It wasn't just the eeriness of the woods, but a deeper feeling—a sense that the case was beginning to intrude upon her own life. Her father's death, the childhood memories that seemed insignificant at the time…all of it was now resurfacing as if to taunt her with questions she wasn't sure she wanted answered.

Adam and an Unwanted Memory

While Evelyn was in the woods, Adam visited an old acquaintance—Victor Chalmers, a local historian who had once worked with his father. Chalmers had a reputation for being eccentric, but Adam knew that if anyone had insights into Briarwood's past, it would be him. As they sat in Chalmers' cluttered study, surrounded by stacks of old books and maps, Adam mentioned the Brotherhood of the Feather.

Chalmers raised an eyebrow. "The Feather, you say? An old tale, older than most realize. The Brotherhood was said to be a group of scholars and mystics, back in the 1800s, who believed in the existence of thin places. They thought certain rituals could open doorways, let things cross over."

Adam felt a chill at the mention of rituals. "Do you think it has anything to do with the murders?" he asked, trying to keep his voice steady.

Chalmers gave a cryptic smile. "It's not the first time death has come to Briarwood in clusters. There were disappearances back in the 1920s, too. Bodies found in the woods, always near those stone circles. Strange marks on the skin, like feathers…"

The words struck a nerve, triggering a memory Adam had long buried—a childhood nightmare of being lost in the woods, running toward a faint light only to find himself surrounded by shadowy figures. He hadn't thought about that dream in years, but now it felt disturbingly real.

Adam's Inner Turmoil

The mention of rituals and old deaths stirred something in Adam—an unease that was deeper than fear, closer to a haunting sense of déjà vu. He realized that he had never truly left Briarwood behind, even during his years away. The town's history had a way of seeping into the lives of those who lived there, shaping their fears and desires in ways they barely understood.

Hale's Fractured Focus

Hale's frustration was mounting as he hit another dead end in the archives. The records from the 1920s that might have shed light on the old deaths were missing, and no one seemed to know where they had gone. As he leaned back in his chair, rubbing his temples, he noticed an old, leather-bound notebook shoved behind a stack of dusty boxes. It didn't appear to be an official record, more like a personal journal.

Flipping through the pages, he found notes about local legends, the Brotherhood, and the stone circles. The writer described strange occurrences: a sensation of being watched, lights in the forest at night, and, disturbingly, a series of sketches that resembled the same crossed feathers symbol.

At the back of the journal, Hale found a map of the woods, with several locations marked with dates and initials. One of the dates coincided with his brother's disappearance years ago.

Hale's Guilt and Determination

Hale's breath caught in his throat as he stared at the map. Lucas had been investigating the same things before he died. The realization struck him hard—his brother had been trying to uncover the same secrets Hale was now pursuing. And Hale hadn't been there to protect him. That guilt gnawed at him, driving him to push harder, even as he felt himself nearing a breaking point.

Evelyn and Adam's Unexpected Connection

Evelyn returned from the woods just as Adam was coming out of Chalmers' study. They met up for a late-night coffee, both exhausted but unable to let the case rest. As they sat in the dimly lit café, sharing their findings, Evelyn felt an unspoken bond growing between them. They were both chasing ghosts, but in different ways.

"You said the Brotherhood believed in doorways," she mused aloud, stirring her coffee absentmindedly. "What if these murders are some twisted attempt to open one?"

Adam leaned closer, his expression serious. "Or keep something closed," he replied. "What if all these deaths are just...covering up something that's been here all along?"

There was a moment of silence as they contemplated the idea. It was absurd, and yet...Briarwood had a way of making the absurd feel strangely possible.

The Emerging Connection Between Evelyn and Adam

The conversation marked a turning point in their relationship. What began as a professional collaboration was turning into a shared obsession. There was an intimacy in the way they discussed the case now, an understanding that went beyond words. It was as though their search for answers was pulling them closer together, even as it threatened to unravel the fabric of their lives.

Chapter 11: Shadows and Echoes

The passage of days in Briarwood felt heavy, each moment laced with an unease that seemed to seep from the very earth. For Evelyn, Adam, and Hale, the investigation was not merely about catching a killer—it had become a journey into the heart of darkness, where their own pasts were being dragged into the light. The slow pace of revelations was maddening, but each small detail brought them closer to the truth, even as it deepened the mystery.

Evelyn Delves into Her Father's Past

Evelyn had always known her father was a complicated man, but the deeper she delved into his work, the more she realized how little she truly understood him. His obsession with folklore and "thin places" had never made sense to her as a child, and now, years later, it felt like a key to understanding the strange events surrounding the case. Her father's notes hinted at rituals that bridged the gap between this world and something else, but there were references she couldn't quite decipher—symbols and phrases that seemed to belong to a language all their own.

Evelyn found herself at the library, poring over her father's old reference books, hoping to find some clue that would tie the symbols to the murders. Among the dusty pages, she came across an entry about "liminal spaces"—places where reality was said to be malleable. There was a list of such locations in Briarwood, including the lake where she had once seen the mysterious figure.

As Evelyn read, a memory stirred—a night when she had woken from a vivid dream of being in the woods, surrounded by people dressed in cloaks, their faces obscured. She remembered the feeling of being watched, but when she had told her father, he had dismissed it as a nightmare. Now, as she considered his notes, she wondered if he had known more than he let on.

Evelyn's Need for Closure

The investigation was becoming more than just a case for Evelyn; it was a quest for closure. She needed to understand not only the deaths in Briarwood but her father's role in this hidden world. The more she uncovered, the more she felt that solving these murders was also a way of coming to terms with her own past.

Adam Faces His Demons

Adam found himself revisiting the places of his youth—the secluded park where he had often played alone, the narrow alleys where he used to race his bicycle, the backroom of his father's old office filled with dusty artifacts. These places held memories that he had long suppressed, fragments of a childhood steeped in secrets.

As he wandered through these familiar spaces, he began to recall moments that had always felt disjointed—his father's hushed conversations with Samuel Graves, the strange symbols he had seen drawn on scraps of paper. One memory, in particular, stood out: a night when he had found his father sitting in the study, staring at an old map of Briarwood with red ink markings that circled the lake and the stone circles in the forest.

Adam couldn't remember what his father had said that night, but the look in his eyes had been one of dread. It occurred to Adam now that his father might have been afraid of what he was uncovering.

Adam's Struggle with the Past

Adam had always sought to escape his family's legacy, to build a life for himself that was free of the strange and obscure interests that had consumed his father. But the case was pulling him back into that world, forcing him to confront not just the past but the person he had become as a result of it. The search for answers had become a way for him to reclaim a sense of purpose, even if it meant facing the darkness head-on.

Hale's Growing Paranoia

The more Hale dug into the case, the more he felt as though the answers were slipping through his fingers. He began to notice patterns in the victims' lives, but they were too obscure to form a coherent picture. It was as if the killer—or killers—were operating just beneath the surface, leaving behind clues that hinted at something greater than mere coincidence. The discovery of the old journal and map had only intensified his obsession.

One night, as Hale was returning to his apartment, he noticed a figure standing at the edge of his street. The man was tall and wore a dark coat, his features obscured in the shadows. Hale slowed his pace, feeling a prickle of anxiety.

The figure didn't move, just watched him, and then, as Hale drew closer, turned and walked away.

The encounter left him rattled. Was it just a coincidence, or was someone watching him? It was easy to dismiss the thought as paranoia, but the feeling of being followed didn't go away.

Hale's Descent into Unease

Hale's confidence in his ability to solve the case was starting to erode. His brother's death had stirred up emotions he wasn't prepared to deal with, and now, as the investigation dragged on, he was haunted by the fear that he wasn't capable of finding the truth. The line between his professional life and his personal grief was becoming blurred, making it harder for him to see the case with clarity.

An Unexpected Lead

Evelyn, Adam, and Hale reconvened at the precinct to share their findings. The atmosphere in the room was heavy with frustration, but also a faint glimmer of hope—they were close to something, even if none of them could yet see what it was.

As they discussed the latest clues, a new lead came in. An elderly woman named Margaret Ashford, a long-time Briarwood resident, had called the station claiming to have seen a man lurking near the old stone circle on multiple occasions. Her description matched the figure Hale had seen on his street.

The three of them decided to visit Margaret to see if she could offer any more insight. When they arrived, she greeted them with a mixture of caution and curiosity. "It's not the first time I've seen him," she said, her voice trembling slightly. "He always comes around when there's trouble in the air…like the town knows something is wrong."

Margaret's words were unsettling, and they suggested a deeper connection between the town's history and the current events. It wasn't just about a series of murders; it was about something that had been festering in Briarwood for generations.

Chapter 12: The Broken Thread

The fog hung heavy over Briarwood as the town awoke to another tragedy. The slow unraveling of the case had taken a darker turn, with a new victim discovered in a place no one expected—a quiet residential street, far from the woods or the stone circles. The victim was Rebecca Connelly, a local journalist known for her interest in old Briarwood lore. Her body was found outside her home, slumped over the steering wheel of her car, the engine still running.

The Scene of the Crime

Evelyn arrived at the scene, her heart sinking at the sight of another body. Rebecca had been only a few years older than her, and she had occasionally written articles about the town's history that Evelyn's father used to clip and keep in a scrapbook. It felt personal, somehow, as though the threads of the case were tangling with the very fabric of her life.

The initial examination suggested Rebecca had died from asphyxiation. The lack of struggle indicated it might have been a poisoning, though there were no signs of the usual substances. What caught Evelyn's eye, however, was the small pendant Rebecca wore around her neck—a charm in the shape of crossed feathers, just like the symbols Evelyn had found connected to the Brotherhood.

The presence of the symbol raised more questions. Rebecca wasn't known to be involved with any secretive groups, at least not publicly. But her work as a journalist could have led her to uncover something dangerous. Had she stumbled onto a truth that someone wanted to keep buried?

Evelyn's Growing Despair

The impact of the investigation was wearing on Evelyn. With every new death, the connection to her father seemed to grow stronger, and the stakes felt higher. The possibility that Rebecca had discovered something about the Brotherhood that tied into the recent murders made Evelyn fear that she, too, was becoming a target.

Adam Investigates Rebecca's Articles

Adam took it upon himself to review Rebecca's articles from the past year, searching for any mention of the Brotherhood, the stone circles, or the thin places. Many of her pieces were benign—profiles of local businesses, human interest stories—but there were a few that hinted at darker undertones. One article, in particular, caught his attention. It was about a series of strange symbols that had appeared in various locations around Briarwood, including near the lake and the old abandoned church. The symbols matched the crossed feathers.

In the article, Rebecca had speculated that the symbols were part of an elaborate prank or perhaps the work of an artist with a taste for the macabre. However, she also mentioned an anonymous source who claimed the markings were connected to an "old Briarwood legend" that involved secret rituals to appease the spirits of the forest.

Adam contacted the editor of the paper, hoping to find out more about Rebecca's source. The editor, however, claimed Rebecca had kept her sources private, even from him. "She was protective of her leads," the editor said. "Especially when she was onto something big."

Adam's Resolved Determination

Adam was struck by how much Rebecca's approach to journalism reminded him of his own attitude toward the investigation—persistent, almost to the point of recklessness. Her death felt like a warning, as if someone were trying to silence those who dug too deep. It made him more determined than ever to find out what was really going on, regardless of the danger.

Hale's Distrust and Confusion

Hale was frustrated by how little the new victim fit into the existing pattern. The previous murders had some tenuous connection to the woods or to folklore, but Rebecca's death in the middle of a quiet street disrupted that thread. It was as if the killer—or killers—wanted to disrupt the investigation itself.

He began to suspect that there might be a copycat, someone who saw the murders as an opportunity to settle their own scores under the cover of a larger conspiracy. Or perhaps Rebecca had been a random target, her death only coincidentally bearing the mark of the crossed feathers. But that idea didn't sit right with Hale; there were too many layers of coincidence for it to be random.

Going back to the journal he had found in the archives, Hale searched for references to local journalists. He discovered an entry from the 1970s written by a reporter named Thomas Mayfield, who had also investigated strange deaths in Briarwood. Mayfield had vanished without a trace shortly after publishing an article about "rituals in the forest."

The name triggered something in Hale's memory. His father had once mentioned Thomas Mayfield as a man who "knew too much." Could there be a connection between the missing journalist from decades ago and Rebecca's murder?

Hale's Struggle with the Investigation

Hale was beginning to question his own instincts. The more he tried to piece together the facts, the more elusive the truth became. He couldn't tell if they were dealing with a single mastermind or multiple killers acting independently but drawn to the same places and symbols. His brother's involvement with the Brotherhood continued to haunt him, as though Lucas's death was the key to everything, yet forever out of reach.

A Break in the Case—But at a Cost

In the days following Rebecca's death, Adam managed to track down a lead—an old acquaintance of Rebecca's named Daniel Price, who had once collaborated with her on an investigative piece. Daniel revealed that Rebecca had been following a new story that involved the recent murders. According to him, Rebecca believed there was a "pattern in the chaos," something she couldn't quite articulate but felt was important.

Daniel provided Adam with some of Rebecca's notes, which contained cryptic references to "fractured echoes" and "hidden voices." There were also sketches of the same crossed feathers symbol found at the scene of her death. One note read: "It's not just a coincidence—it's a chain reaction."

Rebecca's words, "a chain reaction," resonated with Adam. The idea that each murder triggered the next, that they were connected not by motive but by consequence, was an unsettling thought. It implied that there was a hidden hand guiding the events—or perhaps something darker than mere human intent.

Chapter 13: Fractured Patterns

The atmosphere in Briarwood had shifted. There was a restlessness in the air, a sense that something was about to break loose. Evelyn, Adam, and Hale felt it too—a growing urgency, as if the secrets they were uncovering were unraveling at an accelerating pace. Rebecca Connelly's death had shaken the investigation, opening up new lines of inquiry while also deepening the sense of chaos.

A Strange Correspondence

While sifting through Rebecca's belongings, Evelyn discovered a letter that had been tucked away in one of her notebooks. It was addressed to Rebecca but signed only with the initial "L." The letter warned her to "stop digging into old stories," suggesting that her investigation was leading her toward something dangerous. There was a mention of "the fractured echoes," echoing the language in Rebecca's notes, as well as a reference to a place called "The Watchtower."

Evelyn couldn't recall a location by that name in Briarwood, but the phrasing felt familiar, as if it came from the town's folklore or one of her father's books. She made a note to search her father's library for any references to it.

The letter's tone suggested that "L" was someone who knew Rebecca well enough to be concerned for her safety, yet who also seemed to understand the risks she was taking. Evelyn shared this finding with Adam and Hale, who were equally puzzled. Was "L" trying to protect Rebecca, or was it a veiled threat?

Evelyn's Uncertainty

Evelyn struggled with the significance of the letter. It was becoming difficult to distinguish between those who were trying to protect others and those who sought to manipulate the truth. The possibility that "L" might still be out there, watching, only added to her growing paranoia. If "L" had indeed warned Rebecca, then perhaps they had insight into the motives behind the murders, or even knowledge of the Brotherhood's activities.

Adam's Discovery of an Old Photograph

Adam's search for connections led him to the local historical society, where he examined archives of Briarwood's past. In an old collection of photographs, he came across a faded image from the early 1900s. The photograph showed a gathering of townspeople near the lake, and among them was a man standing apart from the group, his face partially obscured. His clothing was distinctive—bearing the same crossed feather symbol as the pendant found on Rebecca.

More startling was the identity of one of the figures standing next to him: Thomas Mayfield, the journalist who had disappeared decades earlier. Seeing Mayfield in this old photograph, alive and apparently involved in some kind of ritual gathering, suggested that he had deeper ties to Briarwood's history than anyone had realized. The same crossed feathers appearing across different time periods implied an organization or a tradition that spanned generations.

Adam couldn't shake the feeling that the man in the background might be more than a mere bystander. His gaze in the photograph, fixed on the camera with a kind of knowing intensity, suggested that he was aware of being observed—almost as if he had left a clue behind deliberately.

Adam's Growing Suspicion

The discovery of the photograph made Adam increasingly suspicious that there was a hidden hand guiding events in Briarwood. The recurrence of the crossed feather symbol, along with Mayfield's mysterious connection to the town's history, hinted at a pattern much older than the current string of murders. He began to wonder if they were dealing with a secret society whose members operated independently, connected only by shared beliefs or rituals.

Hale Uncovers a Forgotten Landmark

Hale's research into "The Watchtower" finally bore fruit when he came across an obscure reference in an old town map. It was a forgotten landmark—an abandoned building located on the outskirts of Briarwood, not far from the stone circle in the forest. The map referred to it as the "Old Bell Tower," a structure that had once been used to signal warnings during times of emergency, but had fallen into disrepair and faded from public memory.

Intrigued, Hale decided to investigate the site. The overgrown path leading to the tower was barely discernible, and the structure itself was in a state of decay, its stone walls covered in moss and ivy. As he ventured inside, Hale noticed markings on the walls—symbols carved into the stone that matched the crossed feathers.

Exploring further, he found a small, dusty room at the base of the tower. There, he discovered a stack of papers, yellowed with age. Among them was an old journal entry describing a ritual held at the tower to "appease the spirits of the woods," along with the names of participants. One name stood out: Lucas Hale.

Hale's brother had been involved in something connected to the old traditions of Briarwood. The realization hit him like a blow, bringing a wave of guilt and confusion. His brother had been linked to the town's dark history in ways he had never imagined. Could his death have been a consequence of his involvement with the rituals? Or was he targeted for trying to leave?

Hale's Internal Struggle

The discovery about his brother deepened Hale's despair. The sense that he had failed to protect his brother was overwhelming, and the idea that Lucas had been part of some secretive ritual only added to the weight of his loss. He began to wonder if uncovering the truth would bring him any peace or merely deepen the wound.

Unsettling Revelations

As Evelyn, Adam, and Hale shared their findings, a new picture began to form—one that suggested Briarwood's history was marked by cycles of violence and ritualistic behavior, with the crossed feathers serving as a recurring motif. The Watchtower, the Brotherhood, and the mysterious figures in the old photographs pointed toward a tradition of appeasement, possibly tied to the "thin places" that Evelyn's father had studied.

The idea of a "chain reaction" took on a new meaning. What if the murders weren't a series of unrelated acts, but part of a ritualistic cycle that drew people into its orbit? Could it be that those involved, willingly or unwillingly, became part of the pattern, each death sparking the next? This possibility suggested a different kind of threat—not just a person, but a phenomenon that seemed to draw the town itself into its grasp.

Chapter 14: A New Lead Emerges

The morning brought with it a heavy mist that blanketed Briarwood, casting an eerie silence over the town. The investigation had reached a critical point where each new lead seemed to contradict the last, and the lines between coincidence and design blurred further. But an unexpected phone call would soon jolt the team out of their mounting frustration.

The Mysterious Phone Call

Evelyn was at her desk in the station, trying to make sense of the clues, when she received a call from a woman claiming to have information about Rebecca Connelly's death. The voice on the other end was shaky, as if the caller was either scared or cold.

"I know something about the symbols," the woman said in a breathless whisper. "But I can't talk here... meet me at Hunter's Bridge tonight, 10 o'clock."

Before Evelyn could ask any questions, the line went dead. The woman's voice had sounded young, possibly a teenager or someone in their early twenties. The urgency and fear in her tone suggested she wasn't calling on a whim. Evelyn debated the risks of going alone, but the potential for a breakthrough was too valuable to ignore.

She informed Adam and Hale, who agreed to set up a stakeout near the bridge, keeping out of sight to monitor the situation in case it was a trap. The bridge was a known spot for teenagers to hang out, but it also had a darker history—it was here that almost fifteen years ago a local girl drowned under mysterious circumstances. The investigation had been closed as an accidental death, but some in Briarwood still whispered about foul play.

The Meeting at Hunter's Bridge

At 10 p.m., the mist had thickened, shrouding Hunter's Bridge in a cold haze. Evelyn waited, her breath visible in the frigid air, as the sound of water rushing below filled the quiet. Adam and Hale kept a discreet distance, hidden among the trees.

Finally, a figure emerged—a young woman, barely out of her teens, with disheveled hair and darting eyes. Her name was Sophie Larkin, a local college student who had known Rebecca through her journalism class. She looked around nervously before approaching Evelyn.

"I don't have much time," Sophie whispered. "Rebecca was working on something... something connected to the old stories about Briarwood." She glanced over her shoulder as if expecting someone to appear. "She showed me a notebook, full of drawings and symbols. She was convinced there was a connection between the symbols, the murders, and the old folklore."

Evelyn listened intently as Sophie explained that Rebecca had become obsessed with finding a pattern that linked the victims, the symbols, and certain locations around town.

According to Sophie, the last thing Rebecca had said to her was, "It's all tied to the Carrington family."

The mention of the Carringtons stirred a memory in Evelyn. The Carringtons had been a prominent family in Briarwood, known for their wealth and influence, but they had become reclusive in recent years. There had also been whispers that the Carrington estate, located near the edge of the woods, held secrets of its own—hidden passages, old maps, and even some strange artifacts.

Adam's Investigation of the Carrington Estate

Intrigued by the new information, Adam decided to look into the Carrington family. He found that the head of the family, Alistair Carrington, had withdrawn from public life after his daughter Olivia's death, and the estate had fallen into a state of disrepair. However, there were rumors that Alistair had been a collector of rare books and artifacts, many of which were said to relate to Briarwood's folklore.

With some persuasion, Adam arranged a meeting with Henry Dawkins, the caretaker of the Carrington estate, who had worked for the family for decades. Dawkins was a reserved man with a graying beard, who spoke in a hushed tone as if the walls had ears.

When Adam inquired about the symbols, Dawkins' demeanor changed subtly—a tightening of the jaw, a quick glance toward the house. "Mr. Carrington was interested in history," he said, "particularly local history. Some of the old stories fascinated him, especially the ones involving the… thin places."

Adam pressed for more details, but Dawkins deflected, stating that any artifacts or books related to those stories had been stored away long ago. However, before Adam left, Dawkins mentioned something peculiar: "There's an old key, hidden in the library. It doesn't open any door in the house."

Hale's Discovery of a Hidden Journal

Meanwhile, Hale had been going through the old police files on Olivia Carrington's death, searching for anything that might suggest a connection to the recent events. He found a reference to a journal that had been taken as evidence but never returned to the family. The journal belonged to Olivia, and its pages contained entries that hinted at her involvement in "something bigger."

The entries spoke of secret gatherings near the stone circles, rituals to "keep the balance," and a fear that she was being watched. There were repeated mentions of a name: "C." Olivia wrote that "C" had told her about "the old ways," and that she had seen the crossed feather symbol etched on the stones during one of these gatherings.

The journal also contained a sketch of Hunter's Bridge, with a note in the margin: "The beginning and the end." Hale couldn't help but wonder if Olivia had known something that connected her death to the current string of murders. Had she uncovered a secret about the Carrington family, or was she merely a victim of the same forces driving the other deaths?

Evelyn, Adam, and Hale Connect the Dots

Evelyn, Adam, and Hale met to discuss their findings. It became clear that the Carrington family was somehow entwined in the town's dark history. Rebecca's mention of the Carringtons, Olivia's cryptic journal, and the mysterious key in the library all pointed toward secrets long buried.

They decided to search the Carrington estate, using the key Dawkins had hinted at. But as they prepared for the next step, a new concern surfaced: what if they were not the only ones trying to unlock the truth? The presence of "L," the repeated appearance of the crossed feathers, and the many strange coincidences suggested that there were others—perhaps even other killers—pursuing their own agendas.

Chapter 15: Echoes from the Past

The fog seemed to cling to Briarwood with a stubborn persistence, creating an almost dreamlike quality to the town. The investigation had begun to feel like chasing shadows, with each clue leading in new and perplexing directions. Yet, a significant discovery lay just ahead, one that would pull the case into unexpected territory.

Uncovering a Pattern in Old Cases

While reviewing cold case files, Hale stumbled upon a report from 1998. The case involved the murder of Daniel Price, a historian and writer who had been working on a book about the folklore and legends of Briarwood. Price's death had been ruled an accident—he had fallen from a cliff near the stone circle—but the circumstances surrounding his death were murky at best.

The detail that caught Hale's attention was that Price had been researching "the thin places" when he died. He had even interviewed members of the Carrington family, particularly Alistair Carrington, about their knowledge of the town's myths. There were hints in the police report that Price believed the legends were tied to real events, even suggesting that some of the old rituals described in his research had survived in secret over the years.

One peculiar note in the file stood out: a mention of a missing artifact. Price had written about a "mirror stone," an object supposedly linked to an ancient ritual involving reflection and sacrifice. The artifact had been believed to reside in Briarwood, but after Price's death, it was never recovered.

The connections between Price's research, the Carringtons, and the current murders seemed too significant to ignore. Hale brought his findings to Evelyn and Adam, suggesting that Price's death might not have been accidental at all.

Hale's Sense of Deja Vu

For Hale, finding this file stirred a sense of deja vu. His brother, Lucas, had also been researching the town's folklore before his own death. The parallel between the two cases was striking—both men had been investigating Briarwood's secrets, and both had met mysterious fates.

The thought made him question if there was a deliberate effort to silence those who got too close to the truth.

A Visit to the Briarwood Historical Society

Determined to learn more about Daniel Price's research, Evelyn and Adam visited the Briarwood Historical Society, where Price had spent much of his time before his death. The society's archivist, Mrs. Wilkins, was a meticulous woman in her sixties who had known Price well. She remembered him as a "man obsessed with the idea that history repeats itself."

"Daniel was convinced that certain events in Briarwood's history kept resurfacing," she explained, her voice tinged with nostalgia. "He believed the same patterns, the same tragedies, happened over and over, each time involving different people but connected by similar symbols and rituals."

Mrs. Wilkins revealed that Price had donated some of his notes to the society, though not all of his materials had been returned after his death. As they sifted through his surviving papers, Evelyn and Adam found a list of names and places, including "The Hollow," a wooded area on the outskirts of

Briarwood, which Price had marked as "a place of transition."

The Hollow was known to locals as an eerie spot, avoided by most after dark. Price's notes described it as one of the "thin places," where the boundary between the physical world and the spiritual realm was said to be particularly fragile. He had written about "echoes" that could be heard there—voices from the past or even glimpses of events long gone.

Among the notes was a peculiar entry: "The Hollow is where it begins... and where it must end." The phrase echoed Olivia Carrington's journal entry about Hunter's Bridge, suggesting a connection between the two locations.

Exploring The Hollow

Later that night, Evelyn, Adam, and Hale ventured into The Hollow, guided by the faint light of the moon and the eerie quiet that surrounded the place. The dense trees loomed overhead, their branches intertwining like fingers, and the air seemed colder the deeper they went.

The Hollow had an unsettling atmosphere, and the trio couldn't shake the feeling of being watched. As they explored, they stumbled upon a small clearing with an ancient stone slab at its center. The surface of the slab was inscribed with strange markings, some resembling the crossed feather symbol, others that were unfamiliar.

Evelyn noticed a faint shimmer on the stone, almost as if the surface was reflecting light that wasn't there. When she touched the stone, a sudden image flashed before her eyes—a fleeting vision of people gathered around the slab, chanting in a language she couldn't recognize. The figures wore dark cloaks, and one of them held a small mirror, directing its reflection toward the stone.

Evelyn's Growing Unease

The brief vision left Evelyn shaken. She had never been one to believe in supernatural forces, yet there was something undeniably unsettling about what she had experienced. The sensation that the stone had retained some fragment of the past felt disturbingly real, as if she had just glimpsed a moment that was still somehow alive.

A New Victim Discovered

Just as the team was about to leave The Hollow, Adam's phone rang. It was a call from the station—another body had been found, this time in a derelict house near Briarwood's outskirts. The victim was identified as Peter Hawkins, a local antiques dealer known for collecting rare and unusual objects. Hawkins was found in a room filled with old books and artifacts, many of them linked to Briarwood's folklore.

Hawkins' death was particularly brutal, with strange symbols carved into the walls around him. The crossed feathers appeared once again, but this time they were accompanied by other glyphs, similar to those on the stone slab in The Hollow. Among Hawkins' possessions was a journal containing notes about Daniel Price's research—he had been looking for the "mirror stone" too.

The timing of Hawkins' death suggested he might have been close to finding something important. His notes indicated that he had recently visited The Old Bell Tower and had arranged a meeting with an unknown person referred to as "The Keeper." The discovery of the term "The Keeper" added yet another layer of mystery—was this a title, a nickname, or a member of some secretive group connected to the ancient rituals?

Chapter 16: Hidden Ties

Peter Hawkins' death cast a shadow over the investigation, leaving more questions than answers. The antiques dealer had lived a seemingly quiet life, but as Evelyn, Adam, and Hale delved deeper, they found that Hawkins had been involved in more than just collecting old objects—he had been a seeker of secrets, with a web of connections that spread far beyond Briarwood.

Discovering Hawkins' Circle

Evelyn and Hale began by interviewing those who knew Hawkins, starting with other local collectors and shop owners. Though many described him as an eccentric who kept to himself, several mentioned that he was a frequent visitor at the Antiquarian Society, a private club in the neighboring town of Redmoor.

The Antiquarian Society was known for hosting monthly gatherings where members would discuss rare artifacts, folklore, and occult topics. Hawkins had attended these meetings regularly, often engaging in heated debates about the authenticity of certain relics and the true origins of local legends.

One of the members, Edgar Mallory, was a retired historian who remembered Hawkins as "a man obsessed with uncovering the past, but also with concealing it." According to Mallory, Hawkins had become fixated on an artifact known as "The Briarwood Amulet," which was rumored to have been used in ancient rituals to protect the town. He had spoken about the amulet often and claimed that it held "the power to see beyond the veil."

Mallory recalled Hawkins' growing paranoia in the months leading up to his death. "He became convinced someone was following him," Mallory said. "He even mentioned something about being 'tested' or 'watched' by a group he referred to as The Guardians."

The Search for The Briarwood Amulet

Intrigued by the mention of the amulet, Adam started looking into its history. The object was believed to have been lost for centuries, but rumors of its existence had resurfaced over the years. There were scattered accounts of the amulet appearing in private collections or being sold at obscure auctions, though its whereabouts had always remained elusive.

Hawkins had apparently been pursuing the amulet for years, collecting books, letters, and any fragments of information that could lead him to it. Evelyn and Hale combed through Hawkins' personal library, finding notes detailing old legends that linked the amulet to "the thin places" around Briarwood, especially The Hollow and the stone circle.

Among Hawkins' belongings, they discovered a letter from an anonymous sender, dated three months before his death. The letter read:

"You are close, but you must tread carefully. The amulet is not just an artifact—it is a key, and keys open doors that should sometimes remain shut. If you find it, remember that not all guardians are benevolent."

The note hinted at something more than just a search for a relic; it suggested a danger tied to the amulet itself. Evelyn wondered if Hawkins had found the amulet, or if he had been killed for getting too close.

A Mysterious Client

Adam followed up on a lead suggesting Hawkins had recently sold some of his lesser-known artifacts to a private buyer. The client, Lydia Ravenscroft, was a collector known for her fascination with esoteric artifacts and folk magic. When Adam met with her at her sprawling manor on the outskirts of Redmoor, Lydia was more than willing to share what she knew about Hawkins.

"I bought a few trinkets from Peter," Lydia explained, her voice as smooth as the silk she wore. "But he was a man who liked to keep his best secrets for himself. We had a… mutual interest in certain items with unique histories, particularly those linked to Briarwood."

Lydia mentioned that Hawkins had contacted her about a month ago, speaking cryptically about an upcoming "revelation." He had hinted at finding the amulet or at least being close to discovering its location. She had even offered to buy it from him should he ever come across it, but Hawkins seemed reluctant to let it go.

When Adam inquired about the crossed feather symbol, Lydia's expression shifted ever so slightly. "Ah, the feather," she said softly. "A sign that dates back to the old ways. It's said to mark the boundary between the living and the dead, a symbol of passage. Some believe it to be a warning, while others see it as an invitation."

Lydia's cryptic insights, while intriguing, did little to clarify Hawkins' death. But before Adam left, she handed him a small wooden box. "He gave this to me a week before he died," she said. "Told me to keep it safe, just in case anything happened to him."

Inside the box was a small, polished stone, no larger than a coin, with a reflective surface. There were faint etchings along the edges, resembling the markings on the stone slab in The Hollow. Could this be a piece of the amulet or something else entirely?

Uncovering an Underground Network

Meanwhile, Evelyn discovered another layer to Hawkins' connections. Through Hawkins' bank records, she found payments to a local man named Gareth Withers, who had a history of smuggling rare artifacts into Briarwood. Withers was known to deal in items that weren't always obtained legally, suggesting that Hawkins' interest in certain relics went beyond innocent collecting.

Evelyn tracked Withers down at a rundown bar near the docks. He was initially resistant to talking, but after some persuasion, he admitted to doing "odd jobs" for Hawkins. "He paid me to find certain things, mostly books and artifacts," Withers said. "But there was one job that felt different—he wanted me to get him a map."

The map, Withers explained, was old—very old—and it supposedly showed the original boundaries of Briarwood. Hawkins had mentioned something about "hidden paths" and "points of convergence." Withers didn't know what the map revealed, only that Hawkins had seemed more nervous than usual after acquiring it.

When Evelyn showed him the crossed feather symbol, Withers hesitated before acknowledging that he had seen it carved into trees and stones in the woods around Briarwood. "There's a rumor," he whispered, leaning in, "about a secret society that uses that mark to guide their way. They call themselves The Veilkeepers."

Chapter 17: Unveiling the Map

After their discussion, the trio decided that locating the map mentioned by Gareth Withers was the next crucial step. It could reveal hidden locations around Briarwood that had been overlooked or provide insight into how the town's past connected to the present murders.

Tracking the Map's Trail

Evelyn and Hale retraced Withers' steps, starting with the antiquities dealer from whom he had acquired the map. The dealer, Oliver Marsh, was an eccentric man who operated from a cluttered shop filled with dusty relics. When confronted with their questions, he initially played coy, but the mention of Hawkins' name made him reconsider.

"Yes, I remember the map," Marsh said, eyeing them cautiously. "It was an old surveyor's map from the late 1700s, depicting Briarwood before the current layout was established. It marked the town's original boundaries and some unusual locations—places that aren't on any modern map."

According to Marsh, Hawkins had been particularly interested in two areas marked on the map: The Hollow and The Old Quarry. The map also featured a peculiar symbol in the corner—a small amulet with an intricate design that resembled crossed feathers and a central reflective stone.

"I sold the map to Hawkins a few months ago," Marsh continued, "but he returned shortly before his death, asking if I had any documents related to the Carrington Estate. He seemed to think the Carringtons had something to do with the places marked on the map."

This revelation tied the Carrington family even more closely to the investigation. The old estate, now mostly abandoned, had once been a grand manor with a labyrinth of cellars and secret passages. Evelyn wondered if the map might be pointing to something hidden on the property.

The Briarwood Amulet's History

As they continued their search, Adam dug deeper into the Briarwood Amulet's origins. The amulet was linked to an ancient ritual known as "The Reflection Rite," a ceremony said to open a gateway between worlds during certain lunar phases. According to legend, the amulet's reflective stone acted as a conduit, allowing glimpses into the past or future. It was believed that during the rite, those who possessed the amulet could communicate with spirits or even influence fate itself.

Further research revealed that the amulet had once been owned by the Carrington family. The last recorded reference to the amulet was in the early 1800s, when Alistair Carrington was rumored to have used it in a ritual to protect his daughter, Olivia, from an illness that threatened her life. There were stories that Alistair had made a pact of some kind during the ritual, exchanging something valuable for Olivia's safety, though the nature of the exchange remained a mystery.

Adam noted that while the amulet had long been thought lost, its appearance in Hawkins' notes suggested otherwise. If Hawkins had indeed located it, it could explain why he was being watched—or even hunted.

Exploring the Carrington Estate

With the map in hand, the trio set out for the old Carrington Estate, hoping to find clues about the amulet or any hidden passages that might be connected to the recent murders. The mansion, though dilapidated, still retained an air of faded grandeur. Tall windows, boarded up from the inside, stared out like the hollow eyes of a skull. Overgrown ivy and creeping vines wrapped around the stone walls, and the iron gates hung ajar, creaking in the wind.

Inside, the estate was a labyrinth of dusty rooms and narrow corridors. Faded portraits of the Carrington ancestors lined the walls, their painted eyes seeming to follow the investigators' every move. Evelyn led the way, following the map's notations toward an area marked as "The Keeper's Room."

The Keeper's Room turned out to be a small chamber concealed behind a false bookshelf. The room was cluttered with old books, ledgers, and artifacts. On a central table lay an aged leather-bound journal, its cover embossed with the crossed feather symbol. The journal, dated 1831, belonged to Alistair Carrington, and contained entries about his research into the amulet and the ritual.

One passage stood out: *"The amulet's power is real, but it is not without cost. The reflection shows what is and what might be, but to see beyond the veil is to invite the darkness in. The key lies in The Hollow, where the veil is thinnest. There, it will open the path."*

The journal confirmed that Alistair had hidden the amulet after using it, concealing it somewhere in or near The Hollow. He referred to a key—possibly another artifact that could help locate or activate the amulet's power.

The Old Key's Connection

As they continued to search the room, Hale found a small, iron key hidden inside a drawer. The key was engraved with intricate designs that matched the symbols on the map. Its age suggested it could indeed be the "key" Alistair had mentioned. Curiously, the key's shape seemed to align with a peculiar indentation on the stone slab in The Hollow—something they had noticed during their previous visit.

Realizing that they might be closer to uncovering the amulet's true location, Evelyn, Adam, and Hale decided to return to The Hollow, armed with the key and the map. However, as they prepared to leave the estate, they were confronted by a shadowy figure standing at the entrance. The figure was cloaked, its face obscured, and it spoke with a calm, authoritative voice.

"You're meddling in matters you do not understand," the figure said. "The amulet is not meant for you, nor for any who seek it. Turn back before it's too late."

Before they could react, the figure disappeared into the darkness, leaving behind an uneasy silence. The warning felt ominously genuine, but they couldn't abandon the investigation now.

Chapter 18: Shadow in the Dark

The warning from the cloaked figure haunted their thoughts as Evelyn, Adam, and Hale left the Carrington Estate. Who was this person, and how did they know so much about the amulet and the investigation? Was this figure simply trying to scare them off, or did they have a deeper role in the unfolding events?

Tracking the Cloaked Figure

Adam decided to start looking into possible connections within Briarwood's underworld. If the figure was aware of Hawkins' activities, perhaps they had been monitoring other residents with an interest in the occult or artifacts. His contacts revealed a whispered rumor about a group known as The Watchers, who supposedly kept an eye on people who delved into forbidden subjects. The Watchers were said to consist of individuals from all walks of life, blending in unnoticed, always observing.

Evelyn and Hale, meanwhile, tried to piece together a profile based on the figure's voice and movements. They spoke with Lydia Ravenscroft again, as her knowledge of Briarwood's secretive circles might yield clues. Lydia mentioned that some within The Antiquarian Society took an oath to guard ancient secrets. She had encountered one such individual years ago who was known only as "The Warden"—a title that implied both protector and enforcer. This person had always worn a cloak and had a reputation for issuing cryptic warnings.

The Warden's identity remained unknown, even to those within the society, but the description matched the figure's demeanor. Evelyn wondered if The Warden had been involved in past incidents where people pursuing the Briarwood Amulet were scared off—or worse.

The Threat Escalates

That night, as Evelyn walked home through the quiet streets of Briarwood, she felt a distinct chill, as if someone were watching her. Her instincts told her she wasn't alone. She quickened her pace, glancing over her shoulder. The streets were empty, but the sense of being followed grew stronger. Suddenly, a figure stepped out of the shadows—a tall, cloaked individual with a hood drawn tightly over their face.

Before Evelyn could react, the figure lunged at her, knocking her to the ground. She managed to fight back, striking at the attacker's ribs with a swift elbow. The assailant stumbled but quickly recovered, pulling out a small, ornate dagger. It gleamed in the moonlight, the blade inscribed with the crossed feather symbol.

Evelyn barely managed to dodge the thrust, twisting away from the blade. Her heart raced as she grabbed a nearby broken bottle from the ground, holding it defensively. Just as the attacker lunged again, a voice shouted from the distance. It was Adam, sprinting towards them.

The figure hesitated for a moment before turning and fleeing into the darkness. Adam reached Evelyn's side, helping her to her feet. She was shaken, but unharmed.

Aftermath and Tension

The near-attack on Evelyn was a stark reminder that they were dealing with someone—or perhaps several people—willing to use violence to protect whatever secrets lay hidden. Adam examined the dagger, noting the intricate design and symbols, which seemed to resemble those on the map and key. The blade was of an older style, suggesting that it could be ceremonial or have a specific purpose beyond mere self-defense.

The attack left Evelyn more determined than ever to unravel the mystery, but it also made her realize how much danger they were truly in. Hale insisted on assigning someone to watch over her and suggested she carry a weapon, as they couldn't afford any more close calls.

As Evelyn recovered from the shock, she received a mysterious letter slid under her door. The letter contained only a single line: *"The veil is thinning, and so is your time."*

Investigating the Attacker

Hale put his resources to work, using his contacts in law enforcement to investigate the cloaked figure. He discovered that there had been other reports over the years of a person dressed similarly, seen near sites associated with Briarwood's local legends. The sightings often coincided with deaths or disappearances of people who were said to be "digging too deep." However, no one had ever managed to identify the figure, and the incidents had been dismissed as rumors or urban legends.

One of Hale's contacts, a retired detective named Arthur Bramwell, had once looked into a case involving a historian who had died under mysterious circumstances while researching Briarwood's folklore. Bramwell remembered that a cloaked figure had been spotted near the historian's home days before his death. He had always believed the case was connected to something larger, but his superiors had closed it quickly, citing a lack of evidence.

The more the trio investigated, the more it seemed that the figure—or perhaps The Warden—had been operating in the shadows for decades, eliminating those who got too close to uncovering certain truths about Briarwood.

Another Threat Looms

The mysterious figure's warning seemed to take on a new significance as Evelyn began to receive more threatening messages. The letters arrived periodically, always containing cryptic phrases hinting at impending danger. One particularly unsettling message read: *"The next will not be a warning."*

The threats extended to Adam and Hale as well. Adam's apartment was ransacked one night, though nothing appeared to be stolen. A message was left scratched into his desk: *"Stay away from The Hollow."*

Hale's situation escalated when his car was tampered with, causing the brakes to fail as he drove down a narrow country road. He managed to avoid a serious accident, but the incident confirmed their fears—someone was actively trying to stop their investigation by any means necessary.

Chapter 19: The Forgotten Case

Arthur Bramwell, now retired, had been a seasoned detective who'd dealt with numerous strange cases during his career, but there was one that had always stuck with him. In 1998, a local historian named Thomas Evers had died under mysterious circumstances. Officially, the cause was listed as accidental drowning in a creek just outside Briarwood, but Bramwell had always suspected foul play. Evers had been researching Briarwood's folklore, particularly the legend of the Briarwood Amulet and the dark rituals associated with it. The day before his death, Evers had confided in Bramwell, hinting that he was on the verge of discovering something that would change everything.

Revisiting the Old Files

Bramwell agreed to meet Evelyn, Adam, and Hale in a small café on the outskirts of town. Though his hair was gray and his movements slower, his mind was still sharp. As they sat down, he spread out a worn leather folder filled with yellowed documents, photographs, and notes from the old case.

"There's a lot that never made it into the official report," Bramwell began. "Evers was terrified in his last days. He kept talking about 'The Warden,' a shadowy figure who was following him. He said this person was connected to a secret society known as The Briarwood Order—a group that protected the town's ancient relics and occult practices."

Evelyn flipped through Bramwell's notes. She found an old photo of Evers taken just days before his death, and a sketch he had made of the amulet's crossed feather design. There were also notes about a sealed crypt beneath an abandoned chapel on the edge of Briarwood, which Evers believed held crucial clues. Bramwell explained that the crypt had been locked for centuries, and there was no official record of anyone being allowed to open it.

"Evers believed there was something in that crypt— documents, maybe even the amulet itself. He was convinced that the Carrington family was involved in keeping the secret," Bramwell said. "I tried to get a warrant to search it back then, but my request was denied. The case was closed as an accidental death, and I was pulled off it."

Discovering Overlooked Evidence

As Bramwell recounted the details, Adam noticed a reference in the notes to a black journal that Evers had kept during his research. It was never found after his death, and there was speculation that it contained critical information about the rituals surrounding the amulet. Bramwell mentioned that Evers' widow, Clara Evers, had kept some of his belongings locked away, never accepting the official story of his death. She had moved to a remote cottage after the tragedy and hadn't been seen in town for years.

The trio decided to visit Clara Evers to see if she still had the black journal or any other relevant items from Thomas's research. Bramwell warned them to tread carefully, as she was known to be reclusive and had turned away visitors in the past.

Clara Evers' Cottage

Clara Evers' cottage was nestled deep in the woods, surrounded by towering pines and thick underbrush. The place had a melancholic charm, with faded lace curtains and a garden that had long gone to seed. The elderly woman who answered the door was frail but had a sharp gaze that seemed to pierce through them.

After a lengthy discussion and reassurances about their intentions, Clara finally allowed them inside. She led them to a dusty attic room where Thomas had kept his research materials. She hesitated before opening an old wooden trunk, explaining that she hadn't touched its contents since his death.

Inside the trunk, they found the black journal, along with a collection of old letters, photographs, and maps. The journal's entries revealed that Thomas had indeed discovered clues about the crypt, the Briarwood Order, and the amulet's potential power. His last entry mentioned a meeting with someone he believed was "The Warden," and that he was on the verge of discovering "the key that unlocks the veil."

Unexpected Revelations

Back at the inn, the trio pored over the journal. One particular entry stood out: *"The Carringtons have been the guardians for centuries. The crypt holds more than bones; it is a vault of secrets. If the veil is truly thinning, the amulet could fall into the wrong hands."* The journal also contained a hand-drawn map that appeared to match the layout of the crypt beneath the chapel, with several hidden compartments marked.

Hale suggested they investigate the chapel under cover of night, fearing that any attempt to go through official channels would alert whoever was trying to keep the secrets buried. As they planned their approach, it became clear that Bramwell's old case wasn't just an isolated mystery—it was the key to understanding the web of murders, secrets, and threats enveloping Briarwood.

Chapter 20: The Crypt Beneath the Chapel

The abandoned chapel stood at the edge of Briarwood, its stone walls covered in moss and ivy, weathered by time. Inside, the air was thick with dust and an eerie silence filled the space, broken only by the creaking of old wooden pews. A large, iron grate in the floor marked the entrance to the crypt. The grate was locked, but the intricate design on the old key matched the engraving on the lock's edge. It clicked open with a rusty groan, revealing a narrow staircase leading down into darkness.

Armed with flashlights and a sense of foreboding, Evelyn, Adam, and Hale descended into the crypt. The stairs seemed to stretch endlessly downward, the temperature dropping with every step. When they reached the bottom, they found themselves in **a** low-vaulted chamber lined with ancient stone sarcophagi. Dusty plaques bore the Carrington family name, and a few had symbols carved into them that matched the design on the amulet.

The Hidden Vault

Following the map from Evers' journal, they located a narrow passage behind a deteriorating wall. The passage led to a hidden vault—a chamber larger and older than the crypt itself. At the far end stood a stone altar, on which rested a large, closed chest adorned with more of the crossed feather symbols and an intricate lock.

As they approached, they noticed faint inscriptions carved into the walls surrounding the chest. The inscriptions were in an archaic form of Latin, and though Evelyn's understanding was limited, she managed to make out a phrase that repeated several times: *"Custos Vehi Transitum"*—"The Guardian Bears the Passage."

Unlocking the Chest

The lock on the chest matched the key they had found at the Carrington estate. With trembling hands, Evelyn inserted the key and turned it. The lock released with a click, and the lid creaked open. Inside, they found ancient scrolls, ceremonial artifacts, and a weathered leather pouch. The pouch contained the Briarwood Amulet, its reflective stone shimmering faintly as if catching light from an unseen source.

But that wasn't all. Beneath the amulet was a stack of letters dating back over a century, detailing the rituals and duties of The Briarwood Order. The letters confirmed that the Carringtons had indeed been the guardians of the amulet, tasked with performing the Reflection Rite to maintain a balance between worlds. The amulet was said to "thin the veil," allowing glimpses of otherworldly knowledge, but only at great risk.

Disturbing Discoveries

While Adam examined the amulet, Hale found a hidden compartment at the bottom of the chest. It contained a small bundle of documents marked with the name Alistair Carrington, including a letter confessing to a dark secret. In the letter, Alistair admitted to using the amulet in a ritual to protect his daughter, Olivia, from an illness. However, there had been a terrible consequence—the ritual had inadvertently opened a doorway that allowed something malevolent to pass through.

The writings suggested that each time the amulet was used, it came with a cost—someone's life was always claimed soon after. This explained the series of deaths that seemed to occur whenever the amulet was disturbed. It also hinted at a connection between the recent murders and an attempt to reactivate the amulet's power.

Suddenly, the faint sound of footsteps echoed from the stairwell. Evelyn's breath caught in her throat. Someone else was in the crypt.

Confrontation in the Dark

The trio quickly extinguished their flashlights, shrouding themselves in darkness. They crouched behind the stone sarcophagi, straining to see who was approaching. A dim light grew stronger as the figure descended, illuminating a cloaked person carrying a lantern. It was the same figure that had attacked Evelyn—the one who had warned them to stay away.

The cloaked figure approached the open chest, their gaze fixing on the amulet. As they reached out to take it, Hale lunged forward, tackling the intruder to the ground. The figure struggled fiercely, pulling out the ceremonial dagger they had used before. Evelyn rushed to help Hale, while Adam grabbed the amulet, holding it away from the fray.

In the struggle, the figure managed to slip free and hurled a small vial of powder onto the ground. The vial shattered, and a thick, acrid smoke filled the chamber, stinging their eyes and making it hard to breathe. By the time the smoke cleared, the cloaked figure had vanished, leaving behind only a scrap of cloth torn from their cloak.

A New Threat Uncovered

The near confrontation left them shaken but more determined than ever. They had uncovered the amulet and the Carringtons' dark history, but it was clear that someone was actively trying to retrieve the amulet for themselves—someone with a dangerous knowledge of its power.

As they regrouped outside the chapel, Evelyn noticed a small symbol burned into the scrap of cloth left behind by the cloaked figure. It was an unfamiliar sigil, distinct from the crossed feathers. They realized that this adversary might not be a lone vigilante but rather a member of a larger, more sinister organization. Perhaps The Briarwood Order had splintered into factions with conflicting purposes—or perhaps there was a new group seeking to harness the amulet's power for their own ends.

Chapter 21: The Carrington Legacy

With the amulet in their possession, Evelyn, Adam, and Hale knew they needed to learn more about the Carrington family's history to understand the true nature of the danger they faced. Alistair Carrington's letter had hinted at a terrible consequence for using the amulet to save his daughter, but it was vague on the details. To uncover the truth, they would need to access the Carrington family archives, which were rumored to be kept in a sealed wing of the old Carrington Manor.

Exploring the Sealed Wing

Carrington Manor loomed large, its imposing Gothic architecture casting long shadows over the grounds. The sealed wing, untouched for decades, was rumored to contain documents and artifacts that had been hidden away due to the dark reputation of certain family members. Evelyn and Adam managed to find a way in through a crumbling section of the exterior wall, while Hale kept watch.

Inside, the air was stale, and dust covered everything like a shroud. As they moved through the abandoned rooms, they found portraits of past Carringtons, some with dark, sorrowful eyes that seemed to follow them. At the end of a long hallway, they discovered a locked door marked with the crossed feather symbol. Using the old key, they unlocked it and stepped into a large study filled with old books, journals, and artifacts—likely the family's private records.

Olivia's Tragic Fate

In the study, they discovered a series of journals belonging to Alistair Carrington, which detailed his daughter Olivia's illness and the lengths he went to save her. Olivia had suffered from a rare, wasting disease that left doctors baffled. Desperate to find a cure, Alistair had turned to the family's old occult practices, ultimately deciding to use the Briarwood Amulet in a ritual known as the Reflection Rite. The ritual was said to "reflect" a person's ailment back to the world beyond the veil, thus purging it from their body.

Alistair's journals recounted how the ritual seemed to work initially—Olivia's symptoms began to fade, and her health improved. But then, things took a darker turn. Olivia started to have nightmares so vivid that she would wake up screaming, claiming to see shadowy figures lurking near her bed. Her behavior grew increasingly erratic, and she began speaking in a voice that wasn't her own, uttering phrases in languages she had never learned.

The final entries in Alistair's journal described Olivia's sudden disappearance. One night, she vanished from her room without a trace, leaving behind only an intricate circle of symbols drawn in ash on the floor. Alistair had spent years trying to find her, convinced that she had been pulled beyond the veil into another realm as a consequence of the ritual.

The Ash Circle

Evelyn and Adam found a photograph in the study showing the circle of symbols that had been left in Olivia's room. They recognized some of the symbols as being similar to the ones found in the hidden compartment of the crypt, but others were unfamiliar. There was a sense that the symbols formed a kind of seal, possibly to contain or summon something.

As they studied the symbols, Adam noticed a pattern connecting them to the sigil burned into the scrap of cloth left behind by the cloaked figure. It suggested that whoever was trying to retrieve the amulet knew about the original ritual and was possibly trying to recreate it—or reverse it.

Discovering More Dark Secrets

Further searching in the study revealed an old family ledger that contained records of payments and unusual expenses. There were several large sums listed as "donations" to a private sanitarium on the outskirts of Briarwood. The payments began shortly after Olivia's disappearance and continued for years. The ledger listed the name Dr. Frederick Lennox, who had overseen Olivia's care before her condition took a turn for the worse. It seemed that Dr. Lennox had been involved in the aftermath of the ritual and possibly knew more about Olivia's fate than Alistair had recorded.

The trio decided that their next step would be to visit the sanitarium, which had closed down years ago. However, records suggested that Dr. Lennox was still alive, living in seclusion. If they could find him, they might uncover what truly happened to Olivia and why the Carrington family had gone to such lengths to conceal it.

A Grim Revelation

Before leaving Carrington Manor, Evelyn stumbled upon a locked cabinet in the study containing a small glass vial with a dried powder residue inside and a note attached. The note read: *"For the final passage."* It appeared to be the same kind of powder the cloaked figure had used to escape from the crypt.

This discovery implied that the powder might have been used in connection with the ritual, possibly to create the ash circles or enhance the effects of the amulet. It also suggested that whoever was trying to retrieve the amulet was familiar with Carrington family secrets and knew exactly how to use the relics and rituals they had uncovered.

Chapter 22: The Abandoned Sanitarium

The sanitarium lay at the outskirts of Briarwood, hidden away in a grove of towering trees. Its faded brick walls were cracked, the windows shattered, and ivy crawled over the neglected structure. A rusted metal gate swung on broken hinges, welcoming Evelyn, Adam, and Hale to a place that had been long forgotten. There was an ominous silence as they entered the grounds, a stillness that seemed to seep from the building itself.

Inside, the corridors were lined with peeling paint and discarded medical equipment, the echoes of distant memories lingering in the air. The trio moved cautiously through the halls, following the faint signs that hinted at the building's former life: faded signs pointing toward patient wards, treatment rooms, and the doctor's offices.

Searching Dr. Lennox's Office

The office once used by Dr. Frederick Lennox was located on the second floor, behind a heavy wooden door that was ajar. Dust covered the old desk, and the shelves were filled with crumbling books and faded medical charts. They began sifting through the contents, looking for any clue that could explain what had happened to Olivia Carrington.

Adam found an old patient file labeled "O. Carrington." It contained medical records, notes from Dr. Lennox, and a series of evaluations documenting Olivia's decline after the ritual. According to the notes, Olivia had exhibited symptoms of dissociation and hallucinations, with recurring episodes where she seemed to speak in other voices or act as though possessed by another presence. Despite these alarming signs, Dr. Lennox's notes indicated that her physical health had continued to improve, almost as if the disease had been transferred elsewhere.

The last entry in her file was dated two days before her disappearance. It mentioned an "experimental treatment" that Dr. Lennox planned to attempt, involving an ancient remedy he had come across in his research—a treatment that required using a substance extracted from the amulet.

The Treatment Room

Following the clues in Olivia's file, they headed toward a sealed treatment room in the basement, where the experimental procedures had taken place. The room had a reinforced door, but with some effort, they managed to force it open. Inside, the air was thick with the scent of mold, and the walls were covered with unfamiliar symbols drawn in charcoal, similar to the ones found in the ash circle at Carrington Manor.

On a rusted metal gurney, they found the remains of a leather-bound journal that appeared to belong to Dr. Lennox. It contained his observations during the final days before Olivia's disappearance. His entries suggested that the experimental treatment had been designed to purge the malevolent influence from her body, but there were signs that the ritual had gone terribly wrong.

The last pages contained frantic scrawls: *"The veil is thinning. She speaks with voices that are not her own. There is something inside her—something that should not be there. The amulet's power is uncontrollable. The guardian must act...before it consumes her completely."*

Dr. Lennox's Whereabouts

Hale found an address scribbled on a scrap of paper tucked inside the journal—likely Dr. Lennox's current residence. It was a cabin in the nearby hills, far from the town. As they prepared to leave the sanitarium, an unsettling sensation washed over them, as though the walls themselves had absorbed the despair of the patients who once walked these halls.

Just before exiting, Evelyn noticed a faint scratching sound coming from behind a boarded-up door at the end of the hallway. Hesitant, she approached and peered through a small gap in the boards. She glimpsed a room filled with rows of old patient beds—and a shadowy figure hunched over, muttering to itself in a low, indecipherable tone. The figure suddenly turned to face her, its eyes wide and unblinking. Before she could react, the door seemed to slam shut on its own, the sound echoing through the deserted building.

The Cabin in the Hills

The journey to Dr. Lennox's cabin was fraught with a tense silence. As they climbed higher into the hills, the air grew colder and the woods more dense. The cabin was a small, solitary structure nestled at the base of a cliff, with smoke curling up from the chimney. When they knocked on the door, a thin, elderly man answered. His eyes were sunken and haunted, but there was a glimmer of recognition when he saw the trio standing before him.

Dr. Lennox was reluctant to talk at first, but after some persuasion, he invited them inside. The cabin was cluttered with books, herbal remedies, and various arcane symbols hanging from the walls. He listened quietly as they recounted their investigation, the rediscovery of Olivia's records, and the events surrounding the Briarwood Amulet.

The Truth Revealed

Dr. Lennox confessed that the treatment had been a desperate attempt to save Olivia. He had been convinced that the amulet's power could be harnessed to "expel" the dark force that had latched onto her. However, the ritual had not gone as planned. As the ceremony reached its climax, something had gone terribly wrong, and a dimensional rift seemed to open briefly in the treatment room, a dark shape emerging from it.

Olivia had vanished in the chaos. Lennox believed that she had been pulled into the rift, possibly taken to the realm beyond the veil that the amulet was connected to. He spent years searching for a way to bring her back but had come to the grim conclusion that there was no way to reverse the effects of the ritual. He had kept silent out of shame and fear of the Carringtons' wrath.

A Dark Realization

Before they left, Dr. Lennox shared one final warning: the rift that had opened during the ritual was not fully sealed, and if the amulet was used again, it could cause the veil to tear completely, allowing entities from the other side to cross over. He urged them to find a way to destroy the amulet or keep it hidden forever, lest it unleash something far worse than what had happened to Olivia.

As they left the cabin, the trio felt a new sense of urgency. The fate of Olivia Carrington might not be as final as it seemed, and the amulet's power was more dangerous than they had imagined. They were not only contending with murderers and ancient secrets but with a supernatural force that defied comprehension.

Chapter 23: At the Hollow Oak Tavern

The Hollow Oak Tavern was a cozy, dimly lit bar on the edge of Briarwood, frequented by locals and travelers alike. It was a place where people could escape the everyday chaos and find a sense of calm. The flickering light from the fireplace cast shadows across the wooden walls, and the air was filled with the comforting aroma of aged whiskey and freshly cooked meals. The trio settled into a corner booth, away from the few patrons scattered about.

Evelyn, Adam, and Hale were nursing their drinks in silence at first, the weight of their discoveries hanging over them. But as the alcohol warmed their senses, they began to open up, peeling back the layers that had remained hidden until now.

Evelyn's Burden

Evelyn took a sip of her whiskey, feeling its heat spread through her chest. "You know," she began, "I wasn't always… on the right side of things. Before Briarwood, I worked as a journalist in the city. I thought I'd make a difference, expose corruption, save people." She chuckled bitterly. "But it turns out, digging too deep has consequences."

She paused, glancing at Adam. "One of my stories uncovered a powerful crime syndicate. I thought it was the break I needed. But they found out before I could publish. My sources vanished… and then, one night, my apartment went up in flames. The fire chief said it was faulty wiring, but I know better."

She swirled the drink in her glass. "I lost everything. Came here to start over, but I guess I can't escape danger. It seems to follow me."

Adam's Regret

Adam leaned back, rubbing a hand over his face. "I get it," he said. "I wasn't a saint either. I spent years as a corporate lawyer, defending clients who deserved to be behind bars. It paid well, but it was hollow work. I wasn't living—I was just… existing."

He took a long drink before continuing. "Then I met someone. Her name was Rachel. She was an artist, full of life, the complete opposite of me. She saw through the façade, you know? Made me feel like I could be someone better. We got engaged, but I got cold feet. Pulled away. I buried myself in work, and one day, she left without a word." His voice wavered. "I still have the engagement ring. Kept it as a reminder of what I threw away."

Evelyn glanced at him with a mixture of understanding and sadness. There was a shared sense of loss between them—different circumstances, but a similar emptiness.

<u>Hale's Hidden Pain</u>

Hale, who had been mostly silent, finally spoke up. "I guess we're all running from something." He gave a half-smile, more of a grimace. "I was in the military. Did a couple of tours. Saw things that… change you. When I got out, I thought I could just go back to normal life. But that's not how it works. Nightmares, flashbacks… they keep pulling you back."

He set his drink down and stared at the table. "My wife, she couldn't handle it. We tried to make it work, but… I wasn't the same person she married. We divorced two years ago. I moved to Briarwood to get away, thinking maybe the quiet here would help me heal." He let out a dry laugh. "But I guess I picked the wrong town for peace."

The Tension Eases

The bar's atmosphere seemed to soften as they shared their stories, the weight of their burdens just a bit lighter now that they had spoken them aloud. There was a newfound understanding between them, a bond forged by shared pain. They weren't just investigating the murders—they were searching for redemption, closure, something to fill the voids in their own lives.

Adam raised his glass. "To lost causes," he said with a wry smile.

Evelyn clinked her glass against his. "To finding answers, even if we don't like what we find."

Hale joined in, his expression softening. "And to the damn fools who keep pushing forward, no matter what."

The glasses came together with a soft clink, the sound carrying a promise—they wouldn't stop now. They had come too far, and there was still so much left to uncover. The bar was just a momentary respite, a place to gather their strength before they plunged back into the darkness that awaited them.

Chapter 24: Diverging Paths

The trio gathered at dawn to discuss their plan. They agreed that time was of the essence; splitting up would be their best chance to piece together the puzzle more quickly.

Evelyn and Adam at Carrington Manor

Evelyn and Adam arrived at Carrington Manor with the first light of morning casting a pale glow over the estate. The mansion loomed before them, its grandeur marred by decay and secrets. They stepped through the main entrance and headed straight to the ballroom, where the ash circles had been found. The air felt heavy with the residual energy of whatever ritual had taken place there.

The ballroom was as they had left it, the faded tapestries lining the walls and the shattered chandelier hanging precariously from above. The ash circles lay undisturbed, etched into the floor with a precision that suggested ritualistic intent.

Examining the Ash Circles

Evelyn knelt by the circles, using a flashlight to inspect the intricate patterns within them. "These symbols," she murmured, "they look like the ones we saw in the sanitarium. Could they be connected to the Briarwood Order's rites?"

Adam scanned the room, his gaze drifting from the circles to the walls, where he noticed faint discolorations in the wood paneling. "Look," he said, walking over to the nearest one. "There are marks here—like something was hung on the walls. Maybe tapestries or artwork. It could be a clue."

He pushed gently against the paneling, and a portion of the wall shifted slightly. Adam pulled back the wooden panel to reveal a hidden compartment containing an old, weathered book. Its leather cover was marked with the same arcane symbols as the ash circles, suggesting it was tied to the ritual they had uncovered.

Evelyn flipped through the book, her eyes widening as she saw that it detailed ritualistic instructions and references to *"The Veil of Realms,"* which supposedly served as a barrier between the physical world and a plane of existence inhabited by otherworldly entities. The rituals described methods to breach the veil, but there were warnings written in the margins: "Do not attempt without the guardian's amulet. Failure to control the rift will result in catastrophe."

Hale's Search for Clues

Meanwhile, Hale delved into Briarwood's archives, hoping to find records on the Briarwood Order and any information about the amulet's history. He started at the town library, combing through old newspapers, town records, and family histories. The more he searched, the clearer it became that the Briarwood Order had been deeply entwined with the town's past.

Hale discovered references to secret meetings held by the Order in various locations, including the abandoned chapel at the edge of Briarwood Forest. He also found a mention of a prophecy regarding the amulet, predicting that it would *"open the gate between worlds in times of great darkness, and summon forth what lay beyond."* It seemed that the Carrington family, along with a few other influential families, had been key members of the Order, using their influence to keep the rituals shrouded in secrecy.

The chapel appeared in several of the documents as a place where *"rites of passage"* had taken place, as well as a rumored "Sanctum of the Amulet." One particularly cryptic entry described a guardian entity linked to the amulet, a being known as "The Watcher," who was said to ensure that no one without the proper knowledge could wield its power.

A Startling Discovery

Back at Carrington Manor, Adam and Evelyn stumbled upon a hidden cellar beneath the ballroom, where more symbols were etched into the stone floor, glowing faintly in the darkness. The cellar was filled with dust-covered artifacts, including a set of ceremonial daggers and a bowl containing what appeared to be dried herbs and crystals.

Among the items, Evelyn found a letter tucked inside an old journal, addressed to Arthur Bramwell. It referenced Olivia's "condition" and an urgent request for Arthur to intervene in the ritual if it got out of hand. The letter hinted that Arthur was once involved in the Briarwood Order's activities and had been designated as a guardian responsible for overseeing the use of the amulet.

Evelyn's pulse quickened as she read aloud: *"If Olivia's suffering cannot be alleviated by the rites, it is your duty to ensure that the amulet remains sealed away. The rift must not be allowed to remain open. Do what you must."*

Hale's Investigation at the Chapel

Hale decided to check out the abandoned chapel, located deep in Briarwood Forest. The building was decrepit, with crumbling stone walls and broken stained-glass windows. Inside, he found an altar covered in dust and tattered tapestries depicting scenes of ritualistic ceremonies. Behind the altar, a small door led down to a crypt-like chamber, where Hale discovered a carved stone pedestal with a shallow depression at the top.

He noticed an inscription in Latin: "*Custos velum, invoca lumen. The guardian of the veil, invoke the light.*" There was also a symbol on the pedestal identical to the one on the amulet. It seemed that this place was connected to the amulet's power and potentially the ritual gone awry that Dr. Lennox had described.

Amidst the dust and decay, Hale found an ancient map tucked inside an alcove behind the altar. The map depicted Briarwood and surrounding areas, with certain locations marked in cryptic symbols. One of the marked sites was Carrington Manor, while others were places Hale had never heard of, but one stood out: "The Forgotten Sanctuary." It was located far beyond the town's borders, in an uncharted region that seemed deliberately omitted from most local maps.

Hollow Oak Tavern

Meeting again at the Hollow Oak Tavern, the trio finds themselves in a familiar corner booth. The atmosphere remains subdued, with the dim light and the murmurs of a few scattered patrons creating a sense of quiet seclusion. Their drinks rest on the wooden table, untouched for the moment as they gather their thoughts. The recent discoveries have cast a dark shadow over their investigation, yet each of them carries a piece of the puzzle.

Sharing Discoveries

Hale speaks first, his voice low but steady. "The chapel was a real find," he begins. "It's clear that the Briarwood Order held some of their rituals there, and it's linked to the amulet. I found a map with marked locations, including Carrington Manor and a place called 'The Forgotten Sanctuary.' There's something about it—it seems like a key location in all of this, but it's far from town."

Adam nods, leaning forward. "Carrington Manor also had more secrets to give up. We found a book in a hidden compartment, and it's filled with details on rituals to breach what they call 'The Veil of Realms.' The ash circles seem to be connected to these rites, and they mention using the amulet as a kind of safeguard to prevent catastrophic consequences." He pauses, exchanging a glance with Evelyn. "There was also a letter to Arthur Bramwell, warning him to intervene if the ritual couldn't heal Olivia. It sounds like he was more involved with the Order than we thought."

Evelyn picks up the thread, her voice tense. "It's possible that Arthur was the guardian mentioned in the book, someone who was supposed to keep the amulet secure. But it seems the ritual either went wrong or didn't have the desired effect. There's talk of 'The Watcher'—some kind of guardian entity tied to the amulet. Maybe it's what the Carringtons tried to summon to help Olivia, but things got out of hand."

Speculating on Olivia's Fate

The group falls silent for a moment, each of them considering the implications of these new details. Adam finally breaks the silence. "If Arthur was supposed to guard the amulet and keep the rift under control, it makes sense why he'd leave town afterward—maybe he was running from his failure. And if Olivia was central to this ritual… could she have been affected by whatever came through that rift?"

Hale frowns, swirling his drink. "Maybe. It's possible she survived the ritual but was changed by it. The letters you found suggest she was suffering from something that couldn't be cured by conventional means." He leans back in his chair. "What if she's still out there, hiding in the shadows of Briarwood, or worse—what if she became something else?"

Evelyn's gaze shifts toward the bar's entrance as if half-expecting to see a figure emerge from the darkness. "It would explain why the Carrington family fell apart afterward. They tried to cover up whatever happened, and the Order disbanded. But if Olivia is still connected to all this, then we're dealing with something much more dangerous than just a secret society."

The Map's Significance

Hale reaches into his coat pocket and pulls out the folded map he found at the chapel, spreading it out on the table. "Here's the thing," he says, pointing to the marked locations. "Each of these places could be significant sites for the rituals or hiding places for artifacts related to the Order. 'The Forgotten Sanctuary' might have the answers we need. If this place was deliberately kept off other maps, then it's important."

Adam traces a finger over the lines of the map, his expression thoughtful. "If that sanctuary was where they performed the most dangerous rites, it could hold evidence of what went wrong with Olivia. But we'll need to be prepared for anything. If these rituals were meant to breach some kind of barrier, then it's not just history we're dealing with—it could be an ongoing threat."

Considering the Next Steps

The discussion shifts back and forth as they analyze the clues, considering the risks and the possibilities. They agree on the need to visit the Forgotten Sanctuary, but there is a lingering concern about what they might encounter there.

Evelyn's voice softens, laced with an uncharacteristic vulnerability. "We're going into the unknown, and this isn't just some ordinary mystery. Whatever happened back then, the people involved kept it secret for a reason. We need to be ready for whatever's out there—whether it's a physical danger or... something else."

Adam places a reassuring hand on her shoulder. "We've come this far. We're not turning back now."

Hale takes a deep breath, the weight of his military training and past experiences settling over him. "We'll go in prepared. But first, let's go over everything one more time, make sure we haven't missed any connections. If the sanctuary is our next move, we can't afford to walk into a trap."

As the conversation winds down, they finish their drinks and stand, each of them bolstered by the sense of unity and purpose. The weight of the investigation may have grown heavier, but so had their resolve. It was clear that the Forgotten Sanctuary was more than just a relic of the past—it was the next step toward unraveling the secrets of the Briarwood Order, Olivia's fate, and the rift that threatened to reshape their world.

The trio leaves the Hollow Oak Tavern with a renewed sense of urgency, each of them aware that their lives are becoming more entwined with the dark history of Briarwood. The next phase of their journey lies before them, and they brace themselves for what the Forgotten Sanctuary may reveal.

Chapter 26: Diverging Paths

As the investigation deepens, the main characters decide to take different directions, each one focused on unraveling the mystery surrounding a specific victim. The evidence, while seemingly fragmented, starts to show hints of a larger pattern—one that ties the victims to a dark, hidden history.

Evelyn's Investigation into Eleanor Cross

Evelyn sits at her desk, surrounded by stacks of Eleanor Cross's research papers and notes on Briarwood's history. Eleanor was known for her meticulous documentation of the town's past, including legends about the Briarwood Order and long-forgotten rituals. Evelyn thumbs through a leather-bound journal, which contains a curious entry about a "curse that befell the Carrington family."

The historian had been researching a period of great unrest in Briarwood, linked to strange disappearances and whispered tales of a dark artifact called the "Briarwood Amulet." As Evelyn sifts through Eleanor's notes, she discovers a connection between the amulet, the Carringtons, and a series of deaths that occurred a century ago—deaths eerily similar to the current murders.

Could Eleanor have uncovered something dangerous, something that made her a target?

Hale's Search for the Truth About Lucas

Hale stands at the old family estate, his mind racing. The weight of his brother's death still lingers heavily on him. Lucas had been troubled in the months leading up to his murder, obsessing over what he called "the family's curse."

Hale flips through some of Lucas's personal belongings: a journal, receipts for trips to Briarwood Forest, and old photographs of the Carrington Manor. He notices one entry in Lucas's journal detailing a late-night meeting with someone called "L." The entry is brief but hints at a secret involving the Hale and Carrington families—something Lucas was desperate to resolve before his death.

Hale begins to suspect that his brother might have uncovered a secret that tied the Hale family to the Briarwood Order, or perhaps even to the rituals themselves. If Lucas's murder was connected to this secret, then Hale's search for answers has just become personal.

Adam Follows Rebecca Connelly's Leads

Adam pores over the articles written by Rebecca Connelly, trying to make sense of her last few weeks of work. The journalist had been investigating a series of mysterious incidents—seemingly unconnected—that had taken place around the time of Falkner's murder. There were hints of ritualistic behavior, strange sightings near Briarwood Forest, and reports of a shadowy figure who was always seen nearby.

As Adam digs deeper, he discovers that Rebecca had started receiving anonymous threats shortly before her death. In one of her last notes, she wrote, "He watches from the shadows, and there's something about 4:17." Adam's stomach tightens as he rereads the time. It's the same as Falkner's frozen watch. Rebecca might have been closer to the truth than anyone realized, which is why she had to be silenced.

Reconnecting the Threads

That evening, the trio regroups at the office, sharing the details of what they've uncovered. A clearer picture starts to form: each victim had some knowledge or connection to a dangerous secret—a secret linked to the Briarwood

Order's rituals and possibly even the Carrington family's dark past. The murders may have been intended to silence those who were too close to revealing the truth.

Evelyn pins a map to the wall, marking the locations associated with each victim. "It's as if the killer is following a specific path or trying to tie up loose ends," she says, her tone resolute. "The amulet, the rituals, the time 4:17… they're all part of the same puzzle."

Hale steps forward, his voice tense. "If that's true, then we need to figure out who's next—and why." He glances at a photograph of Lucas on the board, then looks away, the loss still too fresh.

Adam studies Rebecca's notes, thinking back to her ominous mention of the shadowy figure. "We need to find this person," he says quietly. "If we can uncover their identity, it might lead us to the true motive behind these murders."

As they prepare to split up again to pursue new leads, the atmosphere is charged with urgency. They are getting closer, but each new revelation raises more questions. The next steps will be crucial—because somewhere out there, the killer is already preparing for the next move.

Chapter 27: The Pieces Fall Together

The mood in the office is tense but determined. With each of the main characters focused on their individual investigations, the picture of the case is slowly starting to emerge. However, the deeper they dig, the more it becomes clear that they are not just uncovering a series of murders but an elaborate web of secrets that extends far beyond the current killings.

Evelyn's Discovery About Eleanor Cross

Evelyn spends the day at the town's archives, poring over the documents Eleanor had requested shortly before her death. Among them, she finds a collection of old letters written by members of the Briarwood Order, dating back to the early 1900s. One letter, in particular, catches her eye. It is addressed to a "B.C." and speaks of "the shadow that looms over the Carrington line," along with a reference to the Briarwood Amulet as a "key" to ending the curse.

She also finds records indicating that Eleanor had been looking into Olivia Carrington's mysterious disappearance. The historian had believed that Olivia's fate was linked to the Order's rituals, but there were hints that something went awry—something that the Order tried to cover up. The final entry in Eleanor's notes reads, "The amulet's power lies not just in its history, but in its bearer. The curse was never lifted. It only changed hands."

Evelyn shivers at the implications. Could Olivia Carrington have been the amulet's bearer? If so, what does that mean for the current murders?

Hale's Investigation into Lucas's Connection

Hale follows the clues from his brother's journal to a secluded part of Briarwood Forest, where he finds an old cabin. The place looks abandoned, but as he pushes open the creaking door, he notices signs of recent activity— disturbed dust on the floor, a broken lantern, and a scattering of documents.

Among the papers, Hale discovers a map with the same symbols that were carved on Falkner's palm. There's also a list of names, including Falkner, Eleanor Cross, and Rebecca Connelly. At the bottom of the list is a note written in Lucas's hand: "We are not alone. Someone else knows."

Hale's heart pounds in his chest as the realization sinks in— Lucas had been onto something, but he hadn't been working alone. The implication that there may be multiple people involved in the killings or the rituals changes the stakes. If Lucas was close to uncovering the truth, then his murder wasn't just a warning—it was a silencing.

Adam's Breakthrough in Rebecca's Investigation

Adam follows up on some of Rebecca's notes, visiting the locations where the strange sightings had been reported. One of these locations is an old bell tower on the outskirts of Briarwood. The tower is rumored to have been used by the Briarwood Order in secret gatherings.

Climbing up the spiral staircase, Adam reaches the top and finds remnants of burnt candles, scattered ash, and strange markings on the floor—symbols similar to the ones found at the crime scenes. He also notices scratch marks on the wall near a narrow window that overlooks the entire town. It feels like a perfect vantage point for someone to observe the comings and goings of Briarwood's residents—perhaps even track the victims.

Tucked behind a loose stone in the wall, Adam finds a crumpled piece of paper. It contains a list of times and dates, many of them corresponding to the dates of the murders, including 4:17. It is as if someone had been meticulously documenting the rituals or monitoring the moments of death. Adam's mind races—could the killer have used this place to keep watch, or was it just another misdirection?

A Convergence of Clues

The main characters regroup at the office that evening, and the atmosphere is crackling with tension. Each of them has come back with new information, adding layers to the already complex case. Evelyn lays out the documents she found, explaining Eleanor's belief that the amulet's curse was never truly broken. Hale shares the map he found at the cabin, pointing out that Lucas had uncovered a list of potential victims, which suggests they might still be in danger.

Adam adds his findings from the bell tower. "It's almost like someone was observing the victims," he says, pacing around the room. "The killer might not be working alone—there could be others involved, keeping watch or assisting with the rituals."

Evelyn steps closer to the board, pointing at the photograph of Olivia Carrington. "It keeps coming back to the Carringtons," she murmurs. "The amulet, the curse, the strange events that followed Olivia's disappearance… If we're going to get ahead of this, we need to find out what really happened to her."

Hale's expression hardens with resolve. "We need to dig deeper," he says. "If Lucas was onto something big, then we have to follow his trail, no matter where it leads."

Chapter 28: The Darkness Deepens

The next day, the characters press forward with their separate investigations, each one peeling back a layer of the mystery. Despite their progress, a sense of foreboding hangs in the air. It's as though the closer they get to the truth, the more dangerous the path becomes.

Evelyn's Research Into Olivia Carrington

Evelyn visits the Carrington Manor once again, this time seeking out any personal effects or diaries belonging to Olivia. The housekeeper, an elderly woman who has worked at the manor for decades, reluctantly agrees to show her a small trunk that once belonged to Olivia. Dust-covered and forgotten in the attic, the trunk holds a collection of letters, photographs, and a single tattered journal.

Evelyn begins to read through Olivia's entries, which describe a gradual descent into paranoia. Olivia had been plagued by vivid nightmares, seeing dark figures in the woods surrounding the manor and hearing whispers in the night. One particular entry stands out: "The amulet calls to me. It feels alive. Sometimes I think I can hear it whispering. It must be buried deep, so its power cannot reach anyone again."

The last few entries are frantic, almost illegible, as though Olivia had been writing in a panic. They detail a plan to hide the amulet, mentioning a "crypt of the forgotten". Evelyn's pulse quickens—this amulet could be the key to unlocking the entire mystery. It might hold answers not just about Olivia, but about the murders as well.

Hale's Pursuit of Lucas's Trail

Hale starts contacting the other names listed in Lucas's notes. Most are dead ends, people who have no knowledge of the Briarwood Order or the Carringtons. However, one name leads him to a retired police officer, John Morrissey, who once worked on an old case involving Arthur Bramwell, the disgraced detective.

Morrissey recalls a time when Bramwell was obsessed with the Carringtons, believing them to be at the center of a hidden conspiracy in Briarwood. "He was onto something," Morrissey tells Hale, "but no one would listen to him. Bramwell thought there was a secret society, some kind of ancient order still pulling the strings in this town."

Hale's interest is piqued—Bramwell's old case and the murders his brother was investigating might indeed be connected. Could the "secret society" Bramwell spoke of be the Briarwood Order? And if so, what did they want with the Hale family?

Adam's Search for More Clues About the Bell Tower

Adam returns to the bell tower, determined to find anything he might have missed during his last visit. This time, he brings a metal detector and scans the floor and walls for hidden objects. After a few minutes, the device gives off a series of rapid beeps near the back corner of the room.

Beneath a loose floorboard, Adam finds a small metal box containing a set of keys, an old locket, and a piece of parchment bearing a strange incantation. The keys appear to belong to different locations, one of which has a tag reading "Sanitarium."

His heart skips a beat—could this be referring to the abandoned Briarwood Sanitarium? The locket is engraved with the initials "O.C.," which matches Olivia Carrington's name. It seems the bell tower was more than just a vantage point; it had been used to store items connected to the Carringtons and perhaps even the rituals themselves.

Adam pockets the items and leaves the tower, his thoughts racing. He knows that the sanitarium is tied to the Carrington family's history, but if the keys really do belong there, then he may be about to uncover an entirely new chapter in this dark saga.

Converging Clues and Unsettling Revelations

That evening, the three of them meet once more, this time in a more private setting—Evelyn's home. She spreads Olivia Carrington's journal and the trunk's contents across the coffee table, while Hale and Adam lay out their recent findings. The atmosphere is thick with anticipation as they piece together what they've learned.

Evelyn brings up the crypt mentioned in Olivia's journal. "If the amulet was hidden in the 'crypt of the forgotten,' we need to find out exactly where that is," she says. "It could be beneath the Carrington estate itself."

Hale shares what he learned from John Morrissey about Arthur Bramwell's suspicions. "Bramwell was convinced there was a secret order in Briarwood," he says. "If this is true, the Carringtons and possibly my own family were involved, and Lucas found out something that got him killed."

Adam holds up the locket he found in the bell tower. "This belonged to Olivia," he says. "And the keys—I think one of them is for the old sanitarium. We need to check it out. There may still be records there, or even people who can tell us more about what happened."

As they plan their next steps, the trio agrees to proceed with caution. The crypt, the sanitarium, and Bramwell's old case all hold pieces of the puzzle, and each step forward feels like walking deeper into the darkness.

Evelyn, Hale, and Adam understand that they are closing in on the truth, but they are also aware that the closer they get, the more danger they're in. With each revelation, it becomes clearer that someone—or something—wants to keep the secrets of the Briarwood Order buried in the shadows.

They decide to start with the sanitarium the next morning. It is time to confront the ghosts of Briarwood's past and finally bring light to the darkness that has plagued the town for so long.

Chapter 29: The Weight of New Knowledge

The next morning, Evelyn, Hale, and Adam regroup to plan their return to the Briarwood Sanitarium. Although they had previously explored its corridors, the discovery of the keys Adam found in the bell tower suggests they might have overlooked something vital.

Revisiting the Sanitarium

The trio arrives at the sanitarium in the early afternoon, its decaying façade looming over them like a forgotten specter. Inside, the air is thick with dust and memories. As they retrace their steps, they feel a sense of urgency, knowing that the keys could unlock secrets that have long remained hidden.

Adam begins testing each key on various doors and cabinets, while Evelyn and Hale search for clues they may have missed. Their previous visit had focused heavily on the past, but now they are armed with new information and a clearer understanding of the stakes.

A Hidden Room

After a thorough search, Adam tries one of the smaller keys on a rusted lock at the back of the building. It clicks open, revealing a narrow passageway leading down into a musty storage cellar. As they descend, the air grows colder, and a sense of foreboding settles around them.

At the bottom of the stairs, they find a hidden room sealed off for decades, filled with dusty medical files, old equipment, and patient records. The room looks untouched by time, as if the walls themselves have absorbed the secrets contained within.

At the far end of the room, a heavy metal door stands ominously. Adam uses one of the larger keys, and as the door creaks open, they are met with a chamber that looks nothing like the rest of the sanitarium. It is adorned with faded symbols similar to those found at the crime scenes, but there's an unmistakable aura of dread hanging over it.

Unearthing the Secrets

Evelyn steps forward, drawn to the intricate carvings etched into a stone pedestal in the center of the room. The symbols seem to narrate a tale—a ritual intertwined with the Briarwood Order. Nearby, Hale discovers a drawer filled with old photographs of past patients, some of whom bear striking resemblances to the current victims.

Amidst the documents, he finds a name that sends chills down his spine: "Olivia Carrington." The records reveal that Olivia had been admitted for "psychological evaluation," and there are mentions of a "special treatment" she underwent—a treatment that involved the use of the amulet in experimental procedures.

With a sense of impending revelation, Evelyn speaks up, her voice trembling slightly. "This must connect back to what Dr. Lennox told us. He believed the amulet could expel whatever dark force had latched onto Olivia."

Adam's attention is drawn to a set of keys hanging on the wall, one of which has an engraved number matching a room they hadn't explored before. He suggests they find this room and see if it holds more clues.

A Dark Realization

After some time, they locate the previously unexplored room, Room 23. Inside, they discover a dusty bed, a metal box bolted to the floor, and various remnants of the sanitarium's dark past. When they manage to open the box, they find several items: a cracked mirror, a small journal, and a wooden case containing what appears to be a ceremonial dagger.

As they examine Dr. Lennox's journal, the gravity of his writings begins to sink in. He describes the desperate attempt to save Olivia, convinced that the amulet's power could be harnessed to expel the dark force latched onto her. However, the ritual had gone horribly wrong. "As the ceremony reached its climax, a dimensional rift seemed to open briefly in the treatment room," he wrote, "and Olivia vanished in the chaos."

The room feels stifling as they absorb the implications of what they've read. "Dr. Lennox believed she had been pulled into the rift, possibly taken to a realm beyond the veil," Hale murmurs, his voice barely above a whisper.

Evelyn recalls Lennox's warning, shared in the cabin. "He said the rift was not fully sealed, and if the amulet was used again, it could tear the veil completely. We need to find a way to destroy it or keep it hidden forever."

As they leave the sanitarium, the weight of their discoveries presses heavily upon them. The fate of Olivia Carrington might not be as final as they once thought, and the amulet's power is more dangerous than they had ever imagined.

With each revelation, they understand they are not just contending with murderers and ancient secrets, but with a supernatural force that defies comprehension. They must move swiftly, piecing together the dark tapestry of Briarwood's past before it consumes them all.

Chapter 30: Confronting Shadows

The next day dawns gray and overcast, as if Briarwood itself feels the weight of the darkness stirring beneath its tranquil surface. The team gathers early in Evelyn's office, bracing themselves for what could be the most pivotal day in their investigation.

Morning Preparations

As they review the evidence board, coffee cups in hand, the atmosphere is thick with tension. Maps of the town and its surrounding woods are pinned alongside photographs of the crime scenes, sketches of the strange symbols, and notes from Dr. Lennox's journal. A sense of urgency and dread hangs in the air.

Evelyn draws their attention to the connections they've made: Harold Falkner, Eleanor Cross, Lucas Hale, and Rebecca Connelly, all local figures who delved too deeply into Briarwood's mysteries. "Each victim stumbled upon something forbidden, something that tied them to the Briarwood Order and their experiments."

Adam, who had been silent, speaks up, "It's as if these deaths are a warning or a deliberate attempt to silence those who got too close to the truth."

Hale frowns, his gaze fixed on the photo of his younger brother, Lucas. "If that's the case, why target people who have no obvious connection to each other? Why go to such elaborate lengths to orchestrate these 'ritual' murders?"

Evelyn looks at the board thoughtfully. "Maybe it isn't just about the victims themselves, but about using each murder to point us to the next clue." She taps a faded map of Briarwood on the board, circling a location deep in the woods marked with a symbol they've now come to recognize as a Briarwood Order marker. "This place, near the old Carrington estate—it could hold answers about Olivia's disappearance and why these victims were killed."

A Night Visit

The plan is set: they will investigate the marked location at dusk, under the cover of darkness. As they approach the woods that evening, an unnatural chill fills the air, and the silence feels charged, as if the forest is holding its breath.

As they follow the map, they reach an overgrown trail that leads to an ancient stone structure, partially hidden by foliage. It's small, built like a crypt, and covered in moss and symbols carved into its stone walls. Evelyn examines the carvings, which tell of an ancient ritual that required both the amulet and a "vessel" to act as a bridge to the other side.

Inside the crypt, they find remnants of candles, strange artifacts, and a large stone altar. Hale discovers a locked compartment underneath, and after some searching, Adam locates a loose stone, revealing a keyhole. The key found at Carrington Manor fits perfectly.

The compartment opens to reveal a weathered journal— Olivia Carrington's own diary. Her entries tell of her time at the sanitarium, her fascination with the amulet's power, and the growing sense that she was being drawn into something she couldn't escape.

Olivia's Revelation

Evelyn reads one of the final entries aloud, her voice barely a whisper. "They told me I could be the one to harness the amulet's power, to bridge the veil and release those trapped on the other side. I thought it was only a legend. But now, I see… this place isn't just a sanctuary; it's a prison for the lost."

The entry is dated just a week before Olivia disappeared. The realization hits them hard: Olivia had willingly participated in a ritual that she believed would save others, but in doing so, she may have sacrificed herself. Dr. Lennox's ritual had backfired, trapping Olivia beyond the veil.

Hale clenches his fists, rage flaring in his eyes. "All of this—these deaths, this suffering—was the result of people like Lennox playing with forces they didn't understand."

Just as they are about to leave, Evelyn spots a final line scrawled hastily on the last page: "The key lies within the mirror." Evelyn recalls the cracked mirror they had found in Room 23 back at the sanitarium. They had assumed it was just another remnant of the past, but Olivia's words suggest otherwise.

A Call to Action

As they leave the crypt, they realize that time is running out. Each step brings them closer to unearthing the truth about Briarwood and the malevolent forces tied to the amulet. The key in the mirror might be the last piece needed to understand the full extent of the Order's power and how to seal the rift once and for all.

Their journey isn't over yet, and now they know: the final answers lie in the past they're unearthing, and every secret they uncover brings them closer to stopping the darkness threatening to consume them.

But with each new piece, the shadows seem to grow, as if something—or someone—wants to keep the truth buried forever.

Chapter 31: Into the Shadows

With the crypt behind them and Olivia's words fresh in their minds, the group heads back to town, their thoughts consumed by the meaning of her cryptic message. "The key lies within the mirror." The cracked mirror in Room 23 at the sanitarium now feels like a magnet pulling them back to the very place they'd hoped to leave behind.

Returning to the Sanitarium

The sanitarium is eerily quiet as they make their way to Room 23, where Olivia had undergone her final treatment. The mirror rests against the wall, its fractured surface reflecting pieces of their own faces back at them, distorted and unsettling. Hale, his jaw set, approaches the mirror first, running his fingers along its cracked surface.

Evelyn kneels to inspect it from another angle, recalling Olivia's words. "She said 'within the mirror,' but there's nothing behind it."

Adam paces, his eyes scanning the room for something they might have overlooked. "What if 'within' means more than the literal reflection?" He reaches out to tilt the mirror, and with a quick tug, pulls it from the wall. Behind it is a cavity just large enough to fit a small, intricately-carved box.

Evelyn gingerly retrieves the box and examines it. The top is adorned with an etching of the same symbol that was carved into Harold Falkner's palm—the mark of the Briarwood Order. The clasp is shaped like a serpent swallowing its own tail.

Unveiling the Briarwood Legacy

They open the box, revealing a bundle of yellowed letters and a thick, leather-bound journal marked with the Carrington family crest. The journal is meticulously organized, recounting the history of the Briarwood Order, its members, and the dark rituals they conducted.

As they skim through, a chilling pattern emerges. The Order believed in sacrificing individuals to empower the amulet, with each sacrifice serving as a "beacon" that would draw out otherworldly forces. Hale reads aloud an entry from the early 1900s detailing how members of the Order believed they could harness these powers to "transcend human limitations."

The letters offer a more personal perspective, many of them written by none other than Dr. Lennox. They detail his desperation to save Olivia and the dawning horror as he realized the true purpose of the Order's rituals. He writes of his attempts to break free from the Order but admits that he was too entangled to escape its grip.

Evelyn reads a final letter from Lennox, written the night before the ritual. "If this goes wrong, the consequences will be unimaginable. I can only pray that no one else will pay the price for my folly."

A Growing Darkness

As they process what they've read, the atmosphere in the room shifts, and the air grows cold. A sense of dread fills the room, as though the walls themselves are closing in on them. Evelyn shivers, clutching her arms. "It's almost as if something is watching us… waiting."

Adam nods grimly. "If Dr. Lennox's warning is to be believed, we might be the next ones to pay that price."

Just as they prepare to leave, the door to the room slams shut on its own, and the lights flicker before plunging them into darkness. A low hum fills the air, and they realize they're not alone. Shadows seem to move along the walls, forming vague, humanoid shapes that flicker in and out of sight.

Hale steps forward, his voice steady. "It's trying to keep us from leaving. We need to get out of here before whatever is here crosses over completely."

They struggle against the heavy door, which finally gives way with a loud creak. Bursting into the hallway, they race toward the exit, the oppressive force seeming to follow them, stretching its reach with each step they take.

A Warning in the Shadows

Once outside, they pause to catch their breath. The shadows inside the sanitarium seem to settle, as if retreating now that the group is beyond its walls. Hale turns back to the building, jaw clenched. "Whatever it was, it's growing stronger."

Evelyn grips her own arms, haunted by the memory of the dark shapes. "This thing, this entity—it's not just connected to the murders. It's growing because of them. The more lives it takes, the more it gains a hold in our world."

Adam looks grim. "If we don't act soon, this force could become unstoppable."

They know that time is running out and that their only hope lies in confronting the Order itself—whatever remains of it—and finding a way to neutralize the amulet. With the knowledge they've gathered and Olivia's final words echoing in their minds, they understand that this isn't just about solving a murder. It's about stopping a force far older and more dangerous than they had imagined.

The events of the night have left them shaken but resolute. Armed with the truth about the Briarwood Order and the sacrifices it demands, they brace themselves for the next step.

Chapter 32: Revelations at the Edge of Darkness

The following day, as dawn casts its first pale light over Briarwood, Evelyn, Hale, and Adam reconvene at Carrington Manor. They're determined to unravel the secrets they've uncovered and prepare for what feels like an inevitable confrontation with the unknown.

A Search for Answers

In the study, they spread out all the evidence they've gathered—the maps, the journal entries, and Dr. Lennox's letters. The new revelations from Olivia's diary and the hidden compartment push their understanding forward, but gaps remain.

Adam paces, frustration evident. "We know that the Order needed sacrifices to fuel the amulet's power, and Lennox tried to use it to reach Olivia. But why target Harold Falkner, Eleanor Cross, Lucas, and Rebecca?"

Evelyn taps the edge of the journal thoughtfully. "They each represented something the Order needed: knowledge, power, truth. They were sacrifices not just for their blood but because of what they were trying to unearth. I think that… whatever this thing is, it craves both secrecy and dominance."

Hale's face hardens. "And each time someone got close to the truth, they were silenced."

They're left with an ominous conclusion: the darkness tied to the Order doesn't just demand life; it thrives on despair and secrecy, feeding off the lives of those who draw close to uncovering it. This knowledge only solidifies their resolve, and they decide to pay one final visit to the old Carrington family crypt—where Olivia might have left more answers.

Return to the Carrington Crypt

The afternoon is cloaked in an uneasy quiet as they approach the crypt. Inside, shadows cling to the corners, amplifying the cold as they descend the stone steps. At the center of the crypt lies the cracked altar where they'd previously found Olivia's journal.

Evelyn's hand brushes across the ancient carvings etched into the stone. "She was trying to reach something or someone here, to bring it back. If she didn't intend for Lennox to open the rift, maybe there's a way to close it by reversing what she started."

Hale traces his fingers along a symbol etched into the wall, one that matches the symbol found on the victims. "We might need more than a ritual to close it for good. The amulet itself could be the only thing that seals it… but to do that, we'd have to confront whatever has crossed over."

Adam is skeptical. "Even if that's possible, who's to say the amulet's destruction will truly close the rift?"

Before they can speculate further, Evelyn's gaze falls on a hidden inscription near the altar, partly obscured by dust and age. With a few swipes, she clears the words, barely legible in the dim light: "When the blood of the willing touches stone, the veil shall return."

A chill runs down their spines as they realize what it implies. The crypt might serve as the key, but the ritual requires a sacrifice—a willing one.

Conflicting Choices

Outside the crypt, the tension mounts as the group debates what they've uncovered. Evelyn is determined to end the darkness that has plagued Briarwood, even if it means making the ultimate sacrifice. Hale and Adam, however, are adamant that there must be another way.

Adam grips her arm, his eyes fierce. "You're not doing this, Evelyn. We've lost too much already; I won't lose you too."

Hale's voice is gruff but resolute. "If anyone's going to do it, it should be me. I've lost my brother to this, and I have no family left to mourn me."

Evelyn shakes her head. "This is about more than us. If we're going to stop the Briarwood Order, one of us has to be willing. But I believe there's another way—we just haven't seen it yet."

Despite the charged atmosphere, Evelyn and Adam share a look, an unspoken bond growing stronger with each harrowing step of the investigation. In that moment, they realize how deeply they care for one another, a realization laced with the fear of impending loss.

An Unexpected Revelation

As they leave the crypt, an elderly groundskeeper approaches them, his eyes shadowed with age and secrets. He introduces himself as Elias, a caretaker who's served the Carrington estate for decades.

"I know what you're looking for," he says, his voice gravelly. "The Carrington family has kept its share of secrets, but you won't find them in the crypt alone. Olivia's last wishes—her letters, her final instructions—were entrusted to me. I knew this day would come when someone would try to end what she started."

He hands them a folded letter, brittle with age, addressed to "those who seek the light." Inside, Olivia's words reveal a different interpretation of the ritual: "If the heart is willing, but the blood not spilled, the darkness can still be banished. The true key is not sacrifice, but unity of spirit."

The revelation changes everything. Evelyn, Hale, and Adam realize that perhaps the true "sacrifice" isn't one of life but of commitment and courage—a united willingness to stand together, to confront the darkness without giving in to fear or division

Chapter 33: Unmasking Shadows

The morning after their crypt revelation, Evelyn, Adam, and Hale regroup, determined to confront the familiar faces that now wear an unfamiliar threat. They pore over what they know, re-examining each acquaintance—figures who were once part of their lives in unassuming ways but who now seem enshrouded in deeper mysteries.

Lydia Burns and the Gallery Connection

Their first stop is Lydia Burns's gallery, a place they'd passed by countless times. As they enter, they find the gallery in eerie disarray; paintings are half-covered, as though someone intended to hide or protect them. Lydia is seated behind her desk, startled but attempting to remain calm as they approach.

"Lydia," Evelyn begins, her voice steady but probing. "We know you were close to Harold Falkner, and that you've hosted several of his exhibitions here. Did you ever sense he was... drawn into something beyond the art world?"

Lydia's expression tightens, a subtle shift betraying her calm. "He was. Harold was passionate—too passionate. He spoke about art revealing hidden truths, unlocking the 'veil' as he called it." Her gaze shifts, almost unwillingly, to a painting hung near the back wall.

Evelyn and Adam follow her gaze and recognize the motif from Falkner's crime scene: the eerie slumped figure, symbol on its palm, frozen at 4:17. The realization dawns that Falkner might have used his paintings as cryptic messages, hidden truths he wanted someone to decipher after his death.

An Unexpected Encounter with Martin Wilkes

Leaving the gallery, they decide to find Martin Wilkes, Falkner's former collaborator. He's a writer known for his local histories but recently had shifted to more cryptic, esoteric material. They locate him at his office, where shelves are stuffed with books on the occult and history of Briarwood.

"Martin," Hale addresses him directly. "You worked closely with Falkner. Did he mention anything about his involvement with the Briarwood Order or the amulet?"

Martin chuckles, a dry and oddly unsettling sound. "The Order? You don't just 'mention' them. Harold was entangled in something ancient and dangerous. When he showed me the amulet, I knew it was something we shouldn't touch. I warned him, but he couldn't resist."

Martin's hand twitches toward a drawer, where they catch a glimpse of a silver ring, identical to the one they'd seen on the cloaked figure. Adam reaches out to stop him, demanding an explanation. Martin relents, admitting he once donned the cloak to attend a gathering at the Carrington estate, a secret society meeting that turned ominous when they performed a ritual around the amulet.

Samuel Graves's Patronage and Secrets

That evening, they find Samuel Graves at a dimly lit pub, nursing a drink. Samuel, a long-time supporter of Falkner, seems surprised but unfazed as they approach.

When Evelyn brings up the Order, he sighs heavily. "You don't understand how seductive power can be. Harold wanted to channel something… beyond his art. I thought it was just his eccentricity, but he convinced me it was real." Graves stares into his drink, his voice dropping. "I funded some of his more 'experimental' work, thinking it was all part of his creative genius. But when he showed me the amulet, I knew we'd gone too far."

The group is silent as they absorb Samuel's confession. Each encounter is revealing more of a network of complicity, one that neither Evelyn, Adam, nor Hale had suspected.

Wilkins and Her Ties to the Order's Archives

Mrs. Wilkins, the society's meticulous archivist, is their next visit. As they enter her cluttered office, she looks up, her expression one of weary resignation.

"You've found me at last," she says with a slight smile. "I've spent years preserving the records of this town, watching its secrets remain undisturbed—until now. The Order trusted me to keep the knowledge safe, to protect it."

Adam frowns. "But you knew about the amulet's potential, didn't you?"

She nods. "I did. And I warned them not to use it. But power has a way of whispering to the soul, telling you that you are its rightful keeper."

Mrs. Wilkins hands them an old, dust-laden ledger. Within its pages, they find not only the history of the amulet but also a list of rituals and members, including Falkner's name circled in red. It's clear that the Order's influence is broader and deeper than they imagined.

Lydia Ravenscroft's Unusual Collection

Their final visit is to Lydia Ravenscroft, the esoteric collector. Her house is filled with strange artifacts and a library of rare books. Lydia is different from the others; she seems eager to talk, fascinated by the allure of folk magic and ancient relics.

"The amulet?" She gestures to a row of artifacts. "It's one of the most powerful items I've ever come across. Briarwood's secrets run deep. I've studied the Order, collected relics tied to their practices. But you must understand: the amulet is both a key and a curse. Those who seek to use it often lose themselves."

Adam asks about the cloaked figure they'd encountered. Lydia narrows her eyes. "That wasn't me. But be warned—the Order has protectors, and they're watching you as we speak."

As the group leaves Ravenscroft's home, they're more aware than ever that the threat surrounding them is both real and perilous. Their journey has revealed a tangled web of guilt, secrets, and ambition—those who had touched the amulet in one way or another and paid dearly for it.

But one thing is clear: their enemies are closer than they'd thought, and they are being watched by a shadowed figure wearing a silver ring—a reminder that the Briarwood Order's influence is far from extinguished.

Chapter 34: Unraveling the Past and Present

The atmosphere in the office is tense as Evelyn, Adam, and Hale regroup. With each new discovery, they find themselves pulled deeper into the Carrington legacy, its dark secrets linking not only the Order but the recent victims, Eleanor Cross, Lucas Hale, and Rebecca Connelly, each connected in ways they hadn't foreseen.

The Reappearance of Eleanor's Research

They sift through Eleanor Cross's notes, which Evelyn had recovered from Eleanor's old office weeks prior. Eleanor, a historian, had specialized in Briarwood's forgotten tales, including Carrington's lineage. Her research hinted at an underground society, and in a faded journal entry, she noted a peculiar detail: the Briarwood Amulet was once described as a "veil between worlds."

Evelyn skims Eleanor's notes aloud. "Eleanor believed the amulet wasn't just an artifact but a conduit... something connecting this world to another." The significance of the ash circles at Carrington Manor—and the ritual's outcome—begins to sink in.

Hale, frowning, muses, "If Eleanor had pieced together this much, it's no wonder she was silenced. She was dangerously close to uncovering something monumental about the amulet's influence on Carrington's family."

"If Eleanor was pursuing Olivia's story, then the night Olivia vanished must be tied to the amulet. And if Lennox's warning holds true, maybe the Order wanted to exploit its powers in ways we can't yet understand."

Lucas's Hidden Warning

Lucas Hale, Marcus Hale's brother, was the third victim. Lucas's only apparent connection to the case was his sibling, yet his tragic death hinted at something more sinister. Evelyn recalls a note they had found in Lucas's personal belongings—a page filled with sketches of symbols, one that looked strikingly like the amulet's emblem.

"He must have stumbled upon something," Hale says quietly. "Marcus said Lucas became obsessed with the Order right before his death, claiming he was 'seeing things'—apparitions or shadows in his room at night."

As they examine Lucas's drawings, Evelyn notices an odd pattern, a sequence of symbols leading up to a singular shape—a broken circle. It mirrors the ash circles they found at the manor and is chillingly close to Olivia's last known research symbols, almost as though Lucas had unwittingly been tracing out a ritual.

Adam's face darkens. "It's almost as if Lucas was trying to communicate with someone… or something. Like he was trying to open a path to the same place where Olivia disappeared."

The Journalist's Recordings

Rebecca Connelly, the fourth victim, had been investigating the recent deaths for her newspaper, focusing primarily on Harold Falkner's murder. Evelyn retrieves

Rebecca's voice recorder, which they'd finally managed to access. Rebecca's notes reveal a blend of curiosity and growing fear as she delved into Falkner's past and the Order's possible resurgence.

The recordings are cryptic, with Rebecca mentioning "the silver ring," "strange cloaked figures," and a conversation she overheard about "the heir." One recording, in a hushed voice, is particularly chilling:

"Whoever these people are, they believe in this amulet. They think it holds the answers to everything, from Carrington's secrets to the town's most inexplicable events. But there's someone else too—a shadowed figure they all defer to. The one with the silver ring."

Evelyn pauses the recording, her hand trembling. "She knew the ring-bearer, the same figure we saw. And it sounds like they're all searching for Olivia's lost legacy—the heir to whatever power the amulet holds."

Hale's brow furrows. "The heir… that's why they're coming after people connected to Carrington. They're trying to piece together what's left of her influence, or worse, use it to reopen the rift."

The Carrington Family's Burden

As they assemble all the information on their evidence board, the pieces begin to form a chilling picture. Olivia Carrington hadn't just vanished; she had been at the center of something darker—a web that pulled in not only the Carringtons but unsuspecting individuals like Eleanor, Lucas, and Rebecca. All of them had in some way threatened the Order's efforts to maintain control over the amulet.

The trio stares at the board, where photos of the victims, the amulet, and faded maps of Briarwood and Carrington Manor overlap. They can almost sense Olivia's presence, a looming figure who, despite her absence, has dictated the events unfolding around them.

Adam breaks the silence. "We have to find the last connection—who among these cloaked figures is orchestrating this hunt for the amulet and its heir? Because I'm beginning to think Olivia may have intended to leave her legacy behind for someone."

Evelyn's eyes narrow. "But who? And why would they risk everything, even murder, to protect a truth this horrific?"

With their suspicions now focused on unraveling Olivia's true intentions, the trio decides to retrace her final steps and investigate the rift that Lennox had warned about. Their only lead is to follow the traces she left behind, hoping they might find not only answers but a way to finally put her legacy to rest—or prevent a catastrophe that could tear open the veil between worlds for good.

Chapter 35: Shadows of Carrington

The following morning, the team is back at Carrington Manor, preparing to retrace Olivia's last steps and uncover the truth behind her disappearance. Evelyn, Adam, and Hale gather in the dimly lit study, the air thick with anticipation. Shadows seem to linger in the corners, as if the house itself remembers the night Olivia was lost.

The Secret Room

Guided by Olivia's old notes, they search for a hidden passage rumored to exist somewhere within the study. Hale examines the fireplace closely, running his fingers over its intricate carvings when a hollow click sounds, revealing a narrow door tucked into the wall's paneling.

Inside, they find an aging chamber covered in dust and thick, silent shadows. The walls are lined with shelves holding faded books, ritual objects, and a locked chest in the center of the room. Adam's eyes narrow as he recognizes the Carrington family crest on the chest's lid, surrounded by symbols that match the ash circles from the yard.

"Could this be where Olivia performed the ritual?" Evelyn whispers, her gaze drifting around the eerie room.

Adam moves to the chest and carefully breaks the lock with his knife, lifting the lid to reveal a collection of notes, a velvet-bound journal, and a small vial of black ash. Evelyn takes the journal and begins reading, her face paling as she uncovers more of Olivia's descent into occult practices.

Olivia's Final Days

Olivia's journal is a confessional—a record of her fear and fascination with the Briarwood Amulet and the supernatural forces it seemed to stir. As Evelyn reads, the entries paint a picture of a young woman who was both curious and desperate, searching for a way to rid herself of a darkness that had plagued her dreams.

"'The amulet is a doorway,'" Evelyn reads, "'and I have seen what lies beyond it. They are waiting for me… watching, as if I were their only link to this world.'" The journal goes on to detail a figure she saw frequently in her dreams—a person with a silver ring who whispered promises of power and knowledge.

Adam clenches his jaw. "It sounds like she encountered someone—or something—that saw her as a means of crossing over. Lennox's ritual wasn't just an experiment; it was a last attempt to contain whatever was reaching out to her."

As the team ponders this, Hale notices that the vial of black ash has the same symbol scratched onto its lid that they found carved on Harold Falkner's palm. It's a subtle connection, but it hints that Falkner might have been involved with the Order long before his death.

The Rift and the Cloaked Figure

Just as they're beginning to piece together Olivia's final days, Evelyn spots a figure lurking in the doorway—a dark-cloaked figure with the unmistakable gleam of a silver ring on one hand. The figure slips away into the hall, leaving only the faintest hint of smoky incense in the air.

Without hesitation, they give chase, winding through the manor's halls until they reach the grand staircase. The cloaked figure stops at the top, looking down at them with an air of almost regal menace, before vanishing through a side door that slams shut behind them.

When they finally burst into the room, it's empty. But on a side table, they find a cryptic note left behind:

"You have disturbed the balance. Soon you will understand what lies beyond, as Olivia did. Beware the rift—it waits for you now."

A Grim Realization

They return to the study, shaken by the encounter. Hale is the first to speak, his voice hushed. "This isn't just a mystery anymore. Whatever we're up against, it's something beyond what any of us expected—a force tied to the amulet, the Order, and this rift that claimed Olivia."

Evelyn exhales sharply. "I think we're not just trying to solve a murder; we're on the verge of reopening something that's been dormant since Olivia's disappearance. The ash circles, the rituals, the amulet—it all points to a larger design, something that's been waiting for the right conditions to emerge."

Adam's expression is grim as he studies the note in his hands. "If we push any further, we might be the ones who unleash whatever's been held back. But if we stop now, we may never know the truth about the amulet, Olivia's fate, or who's behind these murders."

Chapter 36: Decisions in the Darkness

The decision to keep digging deeper into Carrington's secrets doesn't come lightly, but Evelyn, Adam, and Hale understand that their own survival—and the truth—depends on uncovering what lies beneath the surface. As they regroup in the study, they pull out the maps, cryptic notes, and images of the amulet that they've collected, determined to trace every remaining clue.

Unearthing the Past

While poring over their materials, Evelyn points to a portion of the Carrington family tree they had previously overlooked. There's an annotation next to Olivia's name, a faded note that reads, "Guardian." Adam and Hale lean in closer, searching for any more details about the term.

Beside it, there's a symbol similar to the one carved into Falkner's palm and seen on the vial of ash.

"This term—it's not just a title, it's a role," Hale observes. "The Order may have chosen Olivia to guard the amulet. But if she was the 'Guardian,' why was she the one to disappear?"

Evelyn nods, her fingers tracing the path of Olivia's line on the family tree. "If Olivia was meant to guard the amulet, perhaps the ritual went wrong because it was trying to separate her from her own purpose. And if that's true, maybe this rift is connected to her, not just the amulet itself."

A Visit from the Unknown

Just as they're putting pieces together, the grandfather clock chimes loudly, echoing through the manor. The sound is unnaturally deep, sending a shiver down their spines. Moments later, the door creaks open, revealing a stranger who stands at the threshold—a tall, thin man with silver-rimmed glasses and a solemn expression.

"Mr. Graves," Adam mutters, recognizing the man as one of Falkner's patrons and a frequent visitor to the gallery.

Graves steps inside, his gaze drifting over the assembled clues on the table, his expression unreadable.

"I was afraid you'd reach this point," he says quietly. "The truth you seek comes with a heavy price. You think this rift took Olivia, but it's far more complicated than that." He looks each of them in the eye, his voice barely a whisper. "I came to warn you, for her sake—and your own."

Adam, tensed and ready, narrows his eyes. "Warn us about what?"

Graves sighs, removing his glasses. "The amulet binds more than just spirits. It binds intentions, the memories of those who sought power but could never control it. Olivia was trying to contain something far older than the Order. But in her attempts, she became a conduit. And now, as you approach the truth, you too may be caught in the snare."

He hands Evelyn a folded piece of parchment with a worn seal that bears the same symbol. "This is the Order's final ritual. It explains how to destroy the amulet. But be warned—it requires the sacrifice of one marked by the amulet."

The Choice Revisited

After Graves departs, Evelyn, Adam, and Hale sit in silence, the weight of his warning heavy in the room. They look down at the ritual instructions, each realizing the possible cost of destroying the amulet and what it might mean for the ones marked by it—Evelyn herself, as her wrist bears a faint, uncanny mark in the shape of the amulet's symbol.

"If we don't destroy it, we'll never stop this cycle. But if we do…" Evelyn's voice trails off, struggling to say the words. She knows what it could mean for her.

Adam places a hand on her shoulder. "There has to be another way. We don't know enough yet. Let's focus on finding more information before we rush into anything."

Hale nods in agreement. "The answers are in this manor. Olivia was close to something; we need to find whatever it was before we decide on our next move."

They resolve to spend the night within Carrington Manor, combing through its rooms and searching for any final clues hidden by time and shadow.

Nightfall and New Revelations

As midnight approaches, Evelyn stumbles upon a passage leading to the long-abandoned west wing of the manor, a section rumored to be Olivia's private quarters. The air is thick with dust, and the silence feels almost oppressive. Adam and Hale follow her, their flashlights casting dim beams that bounce off the walls, revealing old portraits and faint scratch marks along the floor, as if something had been dragged.

In Olivia's room, they find a journal, bound in cracked leather and marked with the same symbol. The entries reveal her thoughts in the days leading up to the ritual, and one particular passage catches Evelyn's eye:

"I am not alone in these halls. He watches from the shadows, his silver ring glinting like a serpent's eye. I thought I knew what I was doing, but this is beyond me. If anyone finds this journal, know that the amulet was not meant for this world."

The trio reads in silence, haunted by Olivia's words. Adam's hand tightens around his flashlight, his knuckles white. "We're dealing with something that's been here long before us. Whatever Olivia faced, she was more afraid of this figure than of anything else."

Hale glances at Evelyn. "The silver ring... it matches Graves' warning. Someone—or something—wants this rift open, but we're the ones standing in the way."

As they leave Olivia's room, a chilling realization dawns upon them: they are not alone in the manor. Shadows flicker in the hall, and a faint sound, like the whisper of an unseen voice, follows them back to the main wing.

With nerves frayed and dread mounting, they decide to barricade themselves in the study for the night. Sleep eludes them, replaced by tense silence and stolen glances at every shadow that moves.

But as dawn approaches, they feel an unspoken determination rise among them. Whatever it takes, they will see this through to the end. The truth of Carrington, the amulet, and Olivia's fate demand resolution, no matter the cost.

Chapter 37: The Choice of Sacrifice

Morning light spills through the dusty windows of Carrington Manor, casting long, slanted beams over the cluttered table where Evelyn, Adam, and Hale sit, exhausted but resolute. The weight of the journal and Graves' warning presses heavily upon them.

A Decision Deferred

Hale breaks the silence, his voice low. "If we choose to destroy the amulet as Graves suggested, it's possible… one of us might have to be the sacrifice." His words hang in the air, and all three feel the severity of the choice ahead.

Evelyn glances at the faint mark on her wrist, a symbol that has somehow become a part of her. "We can't assume anything yet. There might still be something in these notes that shows us another way," she says, turning to Adam, who nods in agreement.

But Adam's gaze shifts to Evelyn's wrist, the unease in his expression unmistakable. "We're dealing with more than just secrets and rituals. This… mark… it's changed you, Evelyn. It may tie you to the amulet in ways we still don't understand."

The group exchanges glances. The choice feels inevitable, but none of them wants to voice it. They gather themselves, determined to continue the search for answers, even if time is running short.

Into the Shadows of Briarwood

With an unspoken understanding, they divide their tasks. Hale takes the lead on tracing the amulet's connection to the Briarwood Order, hoping to understand the rift's purpose. Evelyn and Adam decide to visit the town's archives, focusing on Eleanor Cross's research notes on local legends, rituals, and the supernatural—anything that might shed light on the rift and its effects on Carrington Manor.

In the cramped, dimly lit archives, they sift through Cross's journals. Her notes reveal an obsession with the legends surrounding Briarwood and references to "the Veil" and "the Otherworld," a place described as a shadowed dimension mirroring their own. One entry, dated mere weeks before her death, sends a chill down their spines:

"The Guardian's task is incomplete. The veil grows weaker. Carrington's last heir was meant to seal it, but she was

taken. Those marked by the amulet… they may be our only chance. Or, if they fall, our final curse."

Adam's face pales as he reads the words aloud, the implication settling in. The more they search, the more it seems that Evelyn's connection to the amulet may indeed mark her as a key to the ritual's completion.

Return of the Cloaked Figures

As night falls, they regroup in the study, a quiet tension filling the room. But before they can begin discussing their findings, a loud knock echoes from the main hall. Startled, they freeze, each glancing at the others. Adam motions for them to stay silent, and they wait, breaths held.

The knocking stops, but seconds later, they hear muffled voices outside. Adam peers through the window, his face growing pale. "It's them. The ones in cloaks."

In the moonlight, they can make out the figures shrouded in dark, hooded robes, standing in a line across the yard. They appear to be chanting softly, their faces obscured, but one of them—the tallest—lifts his arm, revealing a hand adorned with a silver ring that catches the light.

Graves.

With steady resolve, Evelyn steps away from the window, her gaze firm. "They're here because they know we're close to unraveling this. They want the amulet, and they'll do anything to get it."

Without a word, Adam and Hale start securing doors and windows, blocking every possible entry point. But as the chanting grows louder, their defenses begin to feel paper-thin. An unsettling sensation seeps through the room, a chill that hints at something beyond human presence.

The Revelation

Suddenly, a loud crash echoes from the back of the house. Evelyn grips the amulet tightly, her heartbeat thudding in her ears. She and Adam exchange a glance, silently agreeing to confront whatever lies beyond the study door. With a nod to Hale, they step cautiously into the hallway, the faint sound of chanting still resonating.

They find themselves in front of a small, hidden door, one they hadn't noticed before. Adam forces it open, revealing a narrow staircase leading down into darkness. The steps are lined with dust, yet the imprint of recent footsteps is unmistakable.

"This could be the final piece," Hale whispers, glancing at Evelyn. They proceed downwards, each step a heartbeat in the dark.

At the bottom, they reach a small room illuminated by a single candle flickering in a corner. In the center stands a stone pedestal, and atop it lies a box covered in runic symbols, sealed with wax. The carvings on the box match the markings on Evelyn's wrist and the amulet, as though it was made to contain it.

Evelyn steps forward, her hand trembling as she places the amulet on the box. The symbols glow faintly, and the air around them grows thick, oppressive.

A voice echoes through the chamber—a familiar one.

"The time has come for you to fulfill your role, Guardian."

Evelyn spins around, the others with her. Standing in the doorway is Graves, his eyes cold, his expression unreadable.

"You bear the mark, Evelyn. You are the last Carrington, and with you lies the power to either seal this rift forever or open it wide and unleash what lies beyond. The choice is yours, but know this: the other side awaits."

A Choice in Shadows

Graves explains the ritual in exacting detail. To destroy the amulet, Evelyn must perform the ritual alone, using her blood to seal the rift. But if the ritual goes wrong, or if Evelyn hesitates, she risks opening the rift completely, allowing entities to cross over into their world.

"It is a sacrifice that requires absolute resolve," Graves warns, his voice thick with urgency. *"One misstep, and you will invite disaster."*

Adam, realizing the danger she's facing, steps forward. "We're not letting you do this alone, Evelyn. We'll find a way to support you, no matter what."

But Graves's gaze shifts to Adam, stern and unyielding. "This is her burden, her inheritance. Only she bears the mark; only she can finish this."

Evelyn stands in the center of the chamber, her hand hovering over the amulet, her breath steady despite the gravity of the moment. Adam and Hale watch from the doorway, ready to intervene, while Graves stands silently, observing, as if awaiting her final decision.

As Evelyn begins the ritual, the air thickens, and a faint hum fills the room. She speaks the incantations Graves instructed, her voice echoing against the stone walls. Light begins to radiate from the amulet, and the rift's faint outline becomes visible—a shimmering, unstable fracture in the very fabric of reality.

The room grows colder, darker, as Evelyn continues, her resolve unwavering. But just as she reaches the final line, an unforeseen force resists her, something strong enough to make her falter. She glances at Adam and Hale, drawing strength from their presence, but as she finishes the last word of the ritual, the rift flickers ominously, and the chamber plunges into silence.

Chapter 38: A Rift Unstable

Silence swathes the small chamber as Evelyn stands motionless, her hand still hovering over the amulet. Adam and Hale strain their ears, listening for any sign, any indication of what the ritual has unleashed—or contained.

Graves, too, stands solemn, his expression guarded, as though he himself isn't certain of what they've done.

A low rumbling fills the room, soft at first, like a distant storm, then growing louder, filling every crevice. The amulet vibrates, emitting an eerie glow that pulses in sync with Evelyn's heartbeat. The walls tremble, and cracks spider across the stone floor beneath her feet, expanding outward from where the amulet sits.

Graves' face hardens. "You may have slowed it… but the rift remains. This is only a temporary seal."

Evelyn stares at him, eyes wide. "Temporary? You said this would close it for good."

Graves' gaze drops to the floor. "It was the only chance we had… with Olivia gone, the connection is incomplete. Only her return could bind the rift permanently."

A sharp intake of breath from Hale echoes around the chamber. "You mean Olivia is alive?" His voice is tight with both dread and hope.

Graves hesitates, glancing between them. "In a way. Trapped, perhaps, in that other realm. But she was pulled there with a purpose—to protect the amulet's power and to maintain the rift. Without her, it will never close."

Evelyn's face darkens. The weight of her family's history and the tragedy of Olivia's fate bear down on her. "There must be a way to retrieve her… if I can enter the rift, maybe I could bring her back." The words escape her lips in a whisper, but her resolve is evident.

Adam steps forward, a flicker of alarm crossing his face. "Evelyn, if you go through that rift, you might not make it back. You have no idea what's on the other side."

Her eyes meet his, fierce and unwavering. "But if I don't, this will never end. The murders, the darkness following us—it will continue to haunt this place, claiming more lives, feeding off whatever lies beyond that rift."

Graves lifts his chin, studying her with an unreadable expression. "You would need an anchor, someone connected to you deeply, to hold the rift steady while you pass through. It is… exceptionally risky. If the connection breaks, you may remain trapped on the other side forever."

Adam's jaw tightens as he looks at Evelyn, the weight of her decision bearing heavily on him. "Then I'll be your anchor. You don't have to do this alone."

Preparing for the Descent

The next night, they gather in the crypt chamber once more, preparing the ritual under Graves's strict instructions. Hale places candles around the perimeter, each one marked with the same symbol as Evelyn's wrist, creating a circle of light. Graves instructs Adam to stay inside the circle, tethered to Evelyn by a piece of red thread that she ties around her wrist, the other end secured around his.

"Remember," Graves warns, his voice steady and low, "once she crosses, you must keep that tether taut. If it loosens, even for a moment, the connection will break, and she'll be lost to the other side."

Adam nods, clutching Evelyn's hand one final time, his gaze unwavering. "I won't let go. No matter what happens."

Evelyn allows herself a fleeting, reassuring smile, her eyes filled with determination. "This is for everyone, Adam. For Olivia. For all of us."

Hale gives her a small, encouraging nod. "We'll be here, waiting for you both."

Taking a deep breath, Evelyn begins the ritual, chanting softly as instructed. The amulet glows with an otherworldly light, casting strange shadows across the walls. As she repeats the incantation, the air grows colder, heavy with an unnatural stillness. Slowly, a shimmering portal, barely visible, materializes before her, crackling with dark energy. With one last look at Adam, she steps forward, disappearing into the void.

The Other Side

The world beyond the rift is like a fractured mirror of their own, veiled in twilight hues and dense fog. Evelyn feels an odd disorientation, as if the ground beneath her isn't quite solid. She's alone, the tether on her wrist an ethereal line connecting her to Adam. The faint light of the tether seems to glow brighter the further she walks, leading her deeper into the mist.

The silence here is absolute, and the landscape eerie, with twisted trees casting elongated shadows that bend and sway as if alive. As she steps forward, she catches glimpses of figures drifting through the fog—shadowy, insubstantial, as though caught between worlds. She recognizes some of them: Eleanor Cross, Lucas Hale, Rebecca Connelly. They wander, their eyes vacant, bound to this place in an endless loop.

Finally, through the thick haze, she sees a small, slender figure at the edge of a dark forest, her back turned, long hair flowing in waves down her shoulders. Evelyn's heart pounds as she approaches, calling out in a voice barely more than a whisper. "Olivia?"

The figure turns, revealing a face so strikingly similar to Evelyn's that it takes her breath away. But Olivia's eyes are distant, haunted, like someone who's been trapped in solitude for far too long. "Evelyn… you shouldn't be here."

Evelyn steps closer, reaching out. "I'm here to bring you back. The rift—it's unstable without you. We need to close it together."

Olivia shakes her head slowly, fear and sorrow etched on her face. "It's too late, Evelyn. This realm… it's already seeped into our world. My fate is sealed. If you try to pull me out, it will tear open the rift entirely."

Desperation fills Evelyn. "There has to be another way. We can finish what Dr. Lennox started and seal this place forever."

A low, guttural growl reverberates through the mist, causing Olivia to stiffen. She glances behind her, a look of terror crossing her face. "They know you're here. You have to leave, now, before they find you."

A Desperate Escape

Just as Evelyn prepares to argue, shadowy forms begin materializing out of the fog, their shapes unnatural and distorted, exuding an ominous energy. Olivia pushes her back. "Run, Evelyn. Get back to the tether—now!"

Evelyn hesitates, torn between saving Olivia and escaping herself. But Olivia's fierce gaze leaves no room for argument. "Go, before they trap you here too. I'll do what I can to keep the rift stable, but you must leave."

With a heavy heart, Evelyn turns and races back through the fog, following the glow of the tether. She can feel the dark figures gaining on her, their whispers like a chilling wind at her back. The ground beneath her seems to shift and buckle, making each step treacherous.

Ahead, she sees the faint glimmer of the portal, and beyond it, Adam's silhouette, his hand reaching through, waiting for her. She leaps, grasping his hand just as the shadowy figures close in around her, and he pulls her through with one final heave.

The Rift Sealed

They collapse on the stone floor of Carrington Manor, breathless and shaken. Graves and Hale rush to their side, helping them up as they recover. The portal flickers and vanishes, leaving only a faint shimmer in the air.

"Did you… find her?" Hale asks, his voice filled with both hope and dread.

Evelyn nods, her expression grim. "She's there, keeping the rift stable as best she can. But she can't come back… and we can't enter that realm again without risking a full breach."

Graves bows his head, a look of resigned sorrow in his eyes. "Then her sacrifice will be remembered. And the amulet…?"

Evelyn clutches it tightly, the cool metal pressing against her palm. "It's a reminder of what's been lost—and what's been saved. Olivia made her choice. Now, we have to live with ours."

Adam places a comforting hand on her shoulder, and together, they exit the crypt, leaving the darkness behind. In the quiet of the early dawn, they know their journey isn't over, but they've taken a step towards healing—and for now, that is enough.

Chapter 39: A Shaken Calm

The dawn seeps into the town, casting pale light over Carrington Manor. After the exhausting ordeal, Evelyn, Adam, and Hale find themselves sharing a rare, quiet moment in the library, each of them grappling with the events that have just transpired. The shadow of Olivia lingers, and the gravity of her sacrifice settles deeply within each of them.

Evelyn sits by the fireplace, her gaze unfocused as she absently traces the contours of the amulet in her palm. Adam watches her, a question he's hesitant to ask hovering on his lips, yet his concern for her is evident in his gaze.

"You know, you don't have to carry this alone," Adam finally murmurs, sitting beside her. "The weight of it all… there's no need to bear it by yourself."

Evelyn offers a small smile, but her eyes remain distant. "It's just… Olivia. The more I learned about her, the more I felt this pull, like some part of me was always bound to her. And knowing that she's…" She trails off, taking a steadying breath. "There's a sense of unfinished business that I can't ignore."

Adam reaches out, gently placing his hand over hers, grounding her. "We'll honor her memory, Evelyn. Together. Whatever that means, whatever it takes."

Across the room, Hale sifts through old Carrington journals, his brow furrowed. "We're close to answers, closer than ever, but this Order—it's clear we've only scratched the surface." He holds up an old notebook filled with scrawling notes. "There's something in here about the Order's practices with symbols and artifacts, about controlling the 'bridge' between worlds."

Evelyn looks up, drawn from her reverie. "Controlling the bridge?"

Hale nods. "From what I can gather, this was a deeply secretive part of the Order's mission. They sought ways to harness and control the veil, almost as if it were a resource. But this amulet was unique in its intensity; they didn't understand the power they were handling."

Adam frowns. "And yet, Dr. Lennox thought he could control it? To close the rift with an artifact like this…"

"Desperation makes people reckless," Hale replies. "He was trying to save her in a way he thought only the amulet could manage. But there are more mysteries within these writings, stories of rituals and testaments that I can barely decipher."

A Dark Omen

Meanwhile, back at the Carrington Manor grounds, Henry Dawkins, the long-standing caretaker, goes about his morning rounds with a heavy heart. He had heard the news from Graves about the night's events, and though he was loyal to the family, a sense of unease had begun to take root. The crypt, the rift, the forbidden connections—all things he had guarded without question—were now fully exposed.

Henry pauses, feeling an odd chill down his spine. The birds are silent, and the usual hum of morning life is absent. He steps closer to the family plot, where the old tombstones rest, and notices something unsettling: fresh ash circles near the tomb of Olivia's mother.

The sight rattles him. As he leans closer, a figure appears behind him—a cloaked silhouette, familiar yet threatening, wearing the same silver ring as before. Henry's heart races as he realizes who it is, but he's silenced before he can utter a word.

In the distance, Graves watches, his expression a mixture of sadness and resignation. He knows that the secrets of the Carringtons and the Order are not so easily extinguished.

Confronting Graves

Back in the library, the trio is startled by urgent knocking at the door. It's Graves, his face pale as he storms into the room, eyes blazing.

"We need to talk," he says, his voice low and fierce. "More than you know has been hidden in that manor, and now it's rising back to the surface. Dawkins... he's gone missing."

The words stun them into silence, and Evelyn feels a pang of guilt. Dawkins, the ever-loyal caretaker, had served her family without question. For him to disappear without a trace felt like a final blow.

"Why didn't you tell us about the Order's plans, or about the extent of the rituals?" Adam demands, his voice sharp. "You knew all along, didn't you?"

Graves nods, visibly weary. "I did, but only pieces. The Order thrived on secrets; even I was not privy to the entirety of their work. They were... they are... zealots of a vision, determined to breach the veil and harness powers we can't even fathom."

Hale steps forward, holding up the journal. "This talks about conduits and sacrifices, about using people as anchors for rituals. Dawkins—was he somehow involved in this?"

A haunted look crosses Graves's face. "Dawkins knew more than anyone. He knew about Olivia's ritual. But he was loyal to a fault, trusted Carrington with his life. If he's gone missing, then I suspect the Order may be looking to continue what they began."

Evelyn feels a chill settle over her, her mind racing. "If Dawkins was somehow bound to this ritual... could they try to reopen the rift using him as a conduit?"

Graves doesn't answer. His silence is confirmation enough.

Uncovering a Final Connection

As the day progresses, Evelyn, Adam, and Hale intensify their search for more information. They comb through every journal, every fragmented note they can find. And it is Evelyn who, by late afternoon, finds a passage in one of the oldest ledgers. She reads it aloud, her voice echoing softly in the quiet room:

"'To bind the veil, one must give what was taken, return what was lost. The tether lies in blood, and in blood it must be repaid. Only then will the realm beyond relinquish its claim.'"

Adam's brow furrows. "A tether in blood... Olivia's bloodline?"

Hale nods slowly. "Or perhaps someone with a deep, binding connection to her. Dawkins had been with the family since she was a child. He was practically family."

Evelyn feels the weight of the amulet grow heavier. "So Dawkins could indeed be the missing piece to the ritual they were attempting. And if the Order has him…"

Graves rises, his expression grave. "They'll try to complete what was started. The only question now is… do we let them?"

Deciding the Next Step

As dusk begins to fall, they gather around the amulet one last time, each of them realizing the gravity of what they face. Destroying the amulet could close the door forever, but if they failed to complete the ritual, the Order could exploit its power.

Evelyn speaks first, her voice steady. "We have to end this for good. No more half measures, no more rituals. We destroy the amulet."

Adam nods. "Agreed. But we need to find Dawkins and ensure that whatever the Order is planning doesn't get a chance to take root."

Hale meets her gaze, and though he is unsure, he stands resolute. "Then let's finish what the Carringtons couldn't."

Graves gives a solemn nod, his voice tinged with regret. "Then prepare yourselves. Destroying the amulet won't be easy. The Order will know we're coming."

As they leave Carrington Manor and step into the deepening night, they know that the battle ahead is unlike anything they've faced before. But the fate of Olivia, and of their own futures, rests on their ability to finally put the darkness to rest.

Chapter 40: The Calm Before the Storm

Morning arrives with an eerie stillness. The events of the past days weigh heavily on Evelyn, Adam, and Hale, and each of them feels the quiet tension of the hours before the final confrontation. They gather at Hale's office, reviewing every piece of evidence, every symbol and cipher they've encountered. Maps, photographs, and scribbled notes clutter the table, the walls now plastered with their findings—a chaotic tapestry of all they've learned about the Order, the amulet, and the town's buried secrets.

Evelyn stares at the center of the display, where a photograph of Olivia Carrington hangs, her expression serene yet haunting, as though she's watching them.

Despite everything, Evelyn feels Olivia's presence urging her forward, as if her fate is tied to this moment.

"It's strange, isn't it?" Evelyn says softly, breaking the silence. "All of this—layers upon layers of secrets, sacrifices, and darkness—all started with people trying to protect what they loved."

Adam nods, pouring coffee for each of them. "Desperation drives people to extreme measures. Even good intentions can turn dangerous."

Hale steps forward, running a finger over the lines on the map that lead to the old chapel deep within the woods, where they believe the Order's members are gathering. "We know where they'll try to complete the ritual," he says. "If we get there before them, we might be able to secure Dawkins, and perhaps we can find a way to destroy the amulet before they get their hands on it."

Evelyn's gaze shifts to the amulet, lying on the table between them. Its dark gemstone gleams in the morning light, seeming to pulse with a life of its own. "But what if it's more complicated than just smashing it? Lennox warned us that even attempting to destroy it could have unintended consequences."

Adam glances at her, a hint of worry in his eyes. "If we don't do something now, they'll use it to open the rift. Whatever happened to Olivia could happen to more people. Maybe even us."

En Route to the Chapel

As they drive out toward the edge of town, the atmosphere inside the car is thick with anticipation. The road twists through the dense woods, each bend seeming to pull them deeper into the unknown. Hale navigates, his eyes sharp on the road, while Evelyn stares out the window, her thoughts drifting between dread and determination. Adam, seated beside her, offers a reassuring smile when he catches her gaze.

"We'll get through this, Evelyn," he says softly. "One way or another."

Evelyn nods, but the tension in her posture is unmistakable. "It feels like… once we do this, there's no turning back. Whatever we uncover, whatever we set free, there's no going back to normal."

"Maybe normal isn't what we're supposed to go back to," Adam replies, a hint of resignation in his voice. "Maybe we're meant to move forward with the truth, whatever it is."

The drive ends at a narrow, overgrown path leading up a slope toward the chapel. The trio exits the car, and as they make their way up the trail, an unnatural chill permeates the air. Shadows flit between the trees, and every crunch of leaves underfoot sounds amplified, their anxiety lending weight to the quiet forest.

The Chapel

They arrive at the chapel just as the first hints of twilight cast long shadows across its crumbling facade. The structure is small and weathered, with ivy creeping over its stone walls and darkened windows giving it a vacant, hollow appearance. The air is thick, almost oppressive, and as they draw closer, they notice faint markings on the chapel's door—symbols they recognize from the Order's documents, inscribed with intent and care.

Hale carefully pushes the door open, and they step inside, greeted by the dim glow of candles scattered throughout the small sanctuary. An eerie calm hangs in the room, and on the far wall, they see a hastily scrawled diagram mirroring the patterns found in the old journals—a ritual design involving the amulet and, at its center, a figure in a hooded cloak.

"Look," Adam whispers, pointing to a small, makeshift altar at the front of the chapel. Resting on it is a journal bound in faded leather, its edges worn and fraying. Evelyn moves closer and picks it up, skimming the pages.

"This must be the Order's journal," she murmurs. "It documents rituals, symbols… everything they used to open the rift. And here," she says, her voice tightening, "instructions for using the amulet to draw a soul across the veil."

Hale's jaw clenches as he studies the words. "They intended to use Olivia as a tether, a sacrificial link to bridge both worlds permanently. Dawkins must have been part of their backup plan—someone they could use if Olivia was lost."

Evelyn closes the journal, her expression steely. "We need to put an end to this, to destroy this knowledge and sever the connection before they arrive."

An Ambush

As they prepare to leave, footsteps echo from behind, and a shadowed figure emerges, blocking their exit. It's Lydia Ravenscroft, the collector they'd seen at the gallery, her usual composed demeanor replaced by a fanatic gleam.

"So you think you can just walk away?" Lydia's voice is sharp, each word tinged with fervor. "You've meddled enough in matters you can't comprehend. The amulet belongs to the Order, as it always has."

Adam steps forward, defiant. "You're trying to finish something that should never have been started. Don't you realize what this will do?"

Lydia sneers. "It will do what it was meant to do—open the path, grant us knowledge, power. Olivia understood that."

Evelyn's eyes narrow. "Olivia never wanted any of this. She was a victim, used and abandoned. This isn't about power; it's about obsession."

Lydia lets out a bitter laugh. "Obsession? It's a sacred duty. You're too blinded by sentiment to understand. But it doesn't matter now." She gestures behind her, and two more figures emerge, cloaked members of the Order, their faces hidden in shadows. One of them holds a ceremonial knife, its blade glinting ominously in the dim light.

Hale, Adam, and Evelyn share a look, steeling themselves for what's to come.

The Final Stand

A fierce struggle ensues, each of them fending off the cultists with everything they have. Adam wrestles the knife from one, narrowly dodging Lydia's strikes, while Evelyn and Hale work together to keep the amulet out of reach. The fight is brutal, and as Lydia lunges for the amulet, Evelyn raises it high above her head, preparing to smash it against the stone altar.

Lydia screams, her voice raw with desperation. "No! You don't know what you're doing!"

But Evelyn is resolute. With all her strength, she brings the amulet down, shattering it into a thousand fragments. A powerful surge of energy erupts, and the entire chapel trembles, an unnatural wind swirling around them as the remnants of the amulet dissolve into wisps of light.

The cultists cry out, clutching at their chests, as if something vital is being torn away. Lydia's face twists in horror as she falls to her knees, the light fading from her eyes.

As the tremors cease, a profound silence falls over the chapel. Evelyn, Adam, and Hale stand amid the wreckage, breathing heavily but unharmed. It's over—the veil, the amulet, the dark connection to the Order. Everything has been severed.

Days later, life in town returns to an uneasy normalcy. The Order is scattered, its remnants disbanded, and no trace of the rift or Olivia's disappearance lingers. The amulet's power is gone, and whatever mysteries it held have been laid to rest. Evelyn, Adam, and Hale find themselves forever changed, bound by a shared history that few would understand.

In the quiet of a crisp autumn morning, they gather once more at the Carrington Manor. This time, there are no questions left unanswered, no lingering fears—just a sense of closure.

As they sit together, watching the morning sun rise over the town, Evelyn finally feels a calm she hasn't known in years. She glances at Adam, a warm smile crossing her lips, and he returns it, the shared burden between them now transformed into a quiet, resilient bond.

They had ventured into darkness and returned, forever marked but undeniably free. The past, with all its secrets and shadows, is behind them, and ahead lies a future filled with possibilities—a chance for healing, for hope, and for peace.

Epilogue: A New Dawn

In the dim glow of the bar, Adam and Evelyn sit close, fingers intertwined on the worn tabletop. The silence between them is comfortable, tinged with a sense of triumph and a rare, almost-forgotten ease. Soft laughter escapes them, their faces relaxed for the first time in what feels like years, as they recount fragments of the past few weeks with an incredulous, almost surreal sense of victory.

Then, the bar door creaks open, and Hale steps in, his figure silhouetted against the streetlights outside. He's holding a small, crisply folded letter. Without a word, he makes his way over to them, his usual air of stoic determination tempered with something almost tentative.

"I thought I'd seen the last of these," he says, setting the letter down on the table. The symbol on the seal—a pair of crossed feathers, meticulously inked—catches the low bar light, and all three fall silent.

Evelyn's fingers brush the symbol, her heart pounding with memories of the dark clues, the figures cloaked in shadow, the endless mysteries. It's the same symbol they saw on rings, cloaks, and scattered notes, binding together secrets they thought had finally been laid to rest.

Adam, feeling the tension creep back into the air, meets Hale's gaze. "Where did you find this?"

"Slipped under my door," Hale replies, his voice low. "No return address. Just... this."

They exchange glances, realizing that perhaps the web they've unraveled is only a part of the whole, a single thread in something much larger than they'd suspected. The envelope sits on the table between them, daring them to open it—but for now, they choose to leave it untouched, its mystery marking the beginning of something yet to come.

In that fleeting moment, they hold onto the comfort of shared laughter and quiet companionship, knowing well that whatever lay within the envelope's confines would soon call them back into the shadows they'd barely escaped.

Printed in Great Britain
by Amazon